Among

M000217682

A novel about the end of days

by

Dominic Peloso

Dark
Mountain
Books

ISBN: 978-1-931468-36-7
First Printing

Day 1:

I awoke with a start, as if some unseen person had just shaken me. My eyes snapped open, tearing the half-encrusted lids apart. Daylight was streaming throughout the room. I was on my side, turned away from the window, but even the reflection of the sun against the wall was so bright that it made me squint. Maybe I'd just been asleep for too long.

I attempted to shift position, still entangled in the covers. The nausea returned. I leaned over the edge of the bed and got sick on the floor. A fever dream of half-remembrances flooded my head, reminding me that I'd been ill, and for some time now. Food poisoning, I think? What did I eat? I couldn't remember the last thing I'd eaten. The sheets felt sticky and damp.

I reached, still half-blind, across to the bedside table. Pushed aside the box of tissues, a half-empty glass of tepid water, and a few other pill bottles, fumbled and grabbed the aspirin. The lid was off. Small red pills tumbled all over the floor and the nightstand and the bedding.

"Fuck."

I reached over, more carefully this time, and turned the alarm clock towards me. It must have become unplugged; dark and dead. I rolled over and shielded my eyes against the direct sunlight. Ugh.

I kicked off the blanket and tried to stand up. Bad idea. The room started spinning. I fell to my knees and got sick a second time. That seemed to do the trick.

1

I staggered back to my feet and sat down on the bed. I held my head in my hands for a long time. The blood started coming back to my brain, and the floor stopped moving up and down in waves. I was on solid ground once again.

I picked through the blankets and found some of the spilled pills. I washed them down with tepid water. Then I got up and stumbled through my apartment into the bathroom. I washed my face in the fresh sink water, and pulled off the stained top I'd been wearing for who knows how long. I looked at my face up close in the mirror. I seemed tired, or older, or broken in some way. My skin didn't look like it fit my skull. I wasn't Elyse; I was an animated skeleton wearing Elyse's skin as a mask. A hot bath might help. I dried my face with a towel. The bathroom seemed a bit off. I couldn't quite put my finger on it. Everything was in its right place, but it seemed... unfamiliar. Like it wasn't the bathroom I had used every day for the past two years, but just a dream of my bathroom. Or maybe I was remembering what my bathroom looked like in a dream and had confused which one was real and which was not.

I went to the living room and pulled on a sweatshirt that I'd previously left draped over the back of the sofa. I pressed the television remote, but the room didn't fill with the sights and sounds of daytime television. I remembered the clock. Power must be out.

Coffee would be good. I had already filled the pot and measured out the grounds before I remembered I just said that the power was out. I opened the refrigerator only to be slapped in the face with the scent of spoiled food. That was enough to make me start heaving for the third time this morning. At least I was standing over the sink.

Day 2:

I spent most of the day sitting on the sofa wrapped in a knitted blanket that my mom made for me when I first told her I was moving out here. I was still too wobbly to actually stand for more than a minute or two, but sitting was fine. The hot bath helped a little, as did a fresh change of clothes into clean sweatpants and comfy socks. The gas was still on, so I had boiled water for tea. Not going to risk any solid food just yet... except for the daily meds. Are pills food? What about cigarettes?

I had work to do; next week's script sat unread and unmemorized on the table. Its cover was now stained with a ring of spilled tea. A novel I'd been meaning to finish for so long that it actually had dust on it had now at least been opened, and the bookmark had progressed a handful of pages towards its conclusion.

A least a dozen times that afternoon I had picked up the remote and realized that the television wasn't going to turn on. And at least a dozen times more I had picked up my phone and realized that the battery was still dead. Kind of wish I could call someone and tell them to bring me some coffee. Or at least tell them I was okay. It was a little surprising that not one person had come by to check on me, especially considering...

I curled back up into the blanket and napped. There was still a dreamlike quality to everything that made me question whether I had just woken up or I had just fallen asleep.

Day 4:

Up. Dressed. Showered. Mascara applied. Feeling, if not 100% at least, I don't know... maybe 85? Good enough to get out and get some real coffee. And maybe some food. The refrigerator had been cleaned, trash thrown down the garbage chute in the hallway. Clothes, if not actually folded, were at least piled neatly in inconspicuous places. I had subsisted on nothing but tea, water, and chips for the last two days. For who knows how long before that I didn't eat anything at all. The bathroom scale showed me down about six pounds. Years ago, when I was home sick one day, I remember my nerdy brother telling me, "best way to lose weight is to contract cholera." Maybe he was right? I think probably it was a joke. What even is cholera anyway? Remember to ask him next time I see him. I had put on a cute pair of jeans that I used to have trouble zipping up. Fit like a glove. Silver lining.

I took my wallet and keys out of the little dish near the door. Scooped up some change, too. I debated leaving the phone, since it wasn't charged, but then I just threw both the phone and the charger in my bag. If they weren't going to get my power on anytime soon, I'd at least be able to get enough juice to check my messages while eating lunch.

Outside, the air was clean, but still and dead. No breeze was blowing. It was only two blocks to the café I frequented. I liked that place mostly because it was close, not because it was good; and because it was a combination of being mildly out of the way enough to always have an empty table, but still had enough foot traffic that I'd get recognized once or twice a month. You say vanity, I say P.R. The more fan photos, the bigger the eventual movie deal.

Omelet? Cheese and mushrooms? Maybe get something less greasy. Stomach was still not as strong as it usually was. Muffin? Kinda carby, but I was already ahead six pounds this week, so maybe treat myself? Or should I lock in the gains? Definitely going to have to take some new publicity photos before the weight comes back, which, let's be honest, it would.

I pulled open the door to the café, but it didn't budge. Then I pushed it, thinking I was an idiot who forgot how to open a door. Didn't budge. Pulled again. I pushed my face up to the glass and shielded my eyes with my hands. It was dark inside, no one was there. I turned and looked up at the sky. The sun was out; it was definitely late enough in the morning that they *should* be open. Out of business maybe? Darn. No matter, there was another café about half a block down that was pretty much the same. The only reason I usually didn't go to that one was because this first one was half a block closer. Half a block... how many extra calories would that burn? Enough to justify an omelet? Nah, probably not.

The second café was dark inside too. There was a handwritten sign taped to the door that said, "Closed early. Sick," in black marker. It was then that I finally noticed; it wasn't quiet and still because there was no breeze, (although there was no breeze that day), it was quiet and still because there were no cars zipping up and down the street. There were no people walking on the sidewalks. There were no smells coming from the restaurants and the car exhausts.

"Hello? Anybody awake?" I said aloud, to no one in particular. The only answer was a crumpled wrapper that tumbled along the sidewalk past my feet. I started walking down the block, paying more attention this time. The first store I passed was closed, and the second, and the third. I started to get confused and worried and anxious. I hadn't brought my anti-anxiety pills with me. I started walking faster, then running. Dark windows and locked doors everywhere. Was it not daytime? No, it was definitely daytime? Holiday? No, even on holidays *some* things are open, right?

The sidewalk in front of the pharmacy was covered in broken glass. The windows were smashed. I stepped over the jagged edges into the store. "Hello?" No answer. The racks of candy bars and shampoo and magazines were untouched. The drug section behind the counter was wrecked and looted. I started biting my nails, for the first time in years.

Gingerly, I stepped back over the glass into the street. In front of the pharmacy was a newspaper box. The headline was visible through the scratched, sun-faded window. "Quarantine Ordered. Martial law takes effect to stem spread of virus." No good. No no no no good. What the hell?

I started walking, then jogging, then running as fast as I could. Not really sure where. Main street? Side street? I ended up in a park I'd never been to before. It was silent except for the slight squeaking coming from the chains of an empty swing set.

"Hello? Police? Army guys?" I said, probably too quietly for anyone to hear, if there had been anyone around to hear, which there wasn't. I remember my dead cell phone just falling from my hand onto the grass. I just stood there for a long time, not even bothering to bend down to pick it up. I wasn't having a panic attack exactly. I know what a panic attack feels like, and this wasn't it. But I had short-circuited. I didn't know what to do next; my body just stopped. And there I stood, stunned, on a deserted street in a deserted city, on a dead world.

Day 5:

Newspapers lay strewn about on the floor of my apartment. All the headlines were pointing to some sort of plague. I remember spending most of that day sitting on my couch, half huddled under that blanket my mom knitted for me, holding a radio that ran on batteries.

"...This is an automated message. Quarantine will remain in effect until the outbreak is under control. All citizens are ordered to return to your homes and wait for assistance from local National Guard units. Do not leave your homes for any reason. If you require food or water, tie a red cloth on your front door and a Guardsman will place a delivery box with subsistence rations on your doorstep. Do not approach the Guardsman or you will be fired upon. This is an automated message. Quarantine will remain in effect..."

Over and over and over again. Stuck on repeat. No one was at the radio station to turn it off. At first, it was just comforting to hear someone's voice, you know? But then it wasn't comforting, because it wasn't *someone's* voice, it was a dead person's voice. A dead person's voice being streamed out across the universe for no one to hear, for only dead people to hear... for only me to hear.

I threw the radio at the wall in frustration. It made a loud noise, and left a dent, and tumbled to the floor. It continued to play the recorded message from behind a potted plant I'd left for dead months ago. I took another swig from a bottle of booze that someone had left at my place after a night out last summer. It tasted like fire and piss. I threw the bottle at the wall. It made a loud noise, and left a dent, and tumbled to the floor.

Talking to myself. Have to self-soothe. "I'm going crazy. I can't be going crazy. Gotta deal Elyse. Gotta deal. Panic attack, oh god, panic attack." Where the fuck was my therapist?

I remember running to the bathroom and grabbing a bottle of pills and gulping a few down. Maybe more than a few. "Happy place. Gotta find my happy place. Breathe...," I repeated to myself. I breathed deeply, staring into the mirror until I convinced myself that my face didn't look like it didn't fit anymore. "That's good," I thought. "At least I don't still look like shit." The distraction gave my panic attack a chance to subside, or at least drop in intensity to the point where it was manageable. Breathe.

I went into the bedroom and took the photo album off the dresser. Back to the sofa, back under the knitted blanket. I ran my fingers across the cover. Handwritten words drawn on the cover in puffy pen years ago, saying, "Happy Place." Flipped it open to a random page, newspaper clippings. Happy place, happy place... Reading out loud, "The award for best new actress in a television series went to Elyse Morgan for her role as Emilia on Malibu Sunset. Remember to breathe Elyse. Happy place..."

I closed my eyes and practiced breathing heavily a few times. Flip the page. Keep reading. Focus on what's in front of you. Focus on what's real and tangible. My fingers slid over the puffy words I'd written on the album cover years ago. Open eyes. Read. "Daytime television became a bit brighter this week with the introduction of Emilia, played by newcomer Elyse

Morgan. Morgan brings a freshness and airiness to what has otherwise been a dismally dull season of Malibu Sunset. Breathe..."

I had brought all my meds out from the bathroom days ago and lined them up on the coffee table. I put the Happy Place book down and reached for the nearest bottle. I remember not even caring which bottle it was. I swallowed a few, and spent the afternoon napping.

Day 8:

It had been about a week since I'd awoken into this nightmare. I remember I was sitting on the floor of the pharmacy with the broken windows, pulling candy bars off the rack, ripping the wrappers apart, and stuffing them in my face. The six pounds had returned by now, probably a lot more. Doesn't matter. My face is covered with chocolate. I didn't get to eat chocolate before. "Always think in the long-term Elyse," people said. Have to consider the consequences. Denied myself so I'd fit into that dress, so I'd look just a tiny bit better in that publicity photo. Here I am in the long-term and there's no one left to give a crap about whether I can button my size 2 jeans. I throw each half-eaten bar out the broken window into the street and open the next one.

There's got to be a million stores in this city, and a million candy bars per store. How many can I eat per day and still have enough to last me the rest of my life? I'm not good at math. Maybe they sell calculators next to the school supplies? Fuck it. Who the fuck cares? I start kicking at the candy rack, trying to tip it over. It's bolted down. I want to vomit.

Day 12:

I was inside the now-darkened, still soulless gym I used to frequent back when it mattered. Enough light coming through the window to see by. Silent. No dumb talk show blaring white noise over the sounds of gears squeaking and lungs grunting. Push it Elyse. Pedal faster, pedal harder. "Work it off work it out work it off work it out..." I shout to no one but myself.

If being here didn't matter, why was I doing it? Was I so used to going to the gym that it was just a habit I couldn't break? There was no one left to impress. No one to be cute for, or to influence into hiring me. There was no reason to keep my heart healthy so I could live a long life surrounded by my grandchildren. If anything, I should start smoking again so I could get this all out of the way faster.

Nothing made sense anymore, and that included me. I didn't make sense anymore. Who was I when taken out of context? Elyse Morgan the actress, the flirty companion, the dutiful daughter, the quirky manic pixie dream girl that lived down the hall. Those were all things I could be in someone else's eyes. But without other people, how do I define myself? Was I at the gym because I needed to be here? No. I was here because I didn't know how to define myself as anything but someone who went to the gym. I felt out of context without other people to define myself in contrast to. So, the easiest thing was to keep being the person people thought I was, even if that no longer mattered.

Pedal faster, pedal harder. "Work it off work it out work it off work it out...."

Day 19:

That morning I was standing in front of my bathroom mirror, washing my face. My eyes looked tired. I started putting on eyeliner out of habit. Better. I was applying lipstick before I realized how pointless this was. I stared at my face, moving closer to the mirror. Lips half pale, dry pink, half bright, wet red. I started smearing the lipstick across my cheek. Back and forth, a mockery of beauty. I looked like a clown.

The tears that came next ruined my eyeliner.

Day 21:

The room was a mess. There'd been a fit. The dresser had been turned over on its side. A mirror smashed and crashed to the floor. I sat in the wreckage of my apartment and cried for a while. What was the point of cleaning things up? I kicked at the debris. Some photographs in now-cracked frames lay on the floor next to me. I picked one up. It was of my family, out at a park somewhere. I must have been like ten at the time. My brother was fourteen or so. My mom looked really happy to have her kids with her in the warm sun. My brother had stuck out his middle finger at the last minute, ruining the picture like he ruined all pictures, like all young boys ruin all pictures. My mom had blacked out his hand with a magic marker and framed the photo anyway. You couldn't really tell at first glance, you had to look close. She said she liked the photo so much she'd rather just edit it than not have that memory at all.

Now here it was, a memory— of a time that no longer existed, of people that were dead and would never be remembered or celebrated by anyone because no one but me was alive to remember or celebrate them. And there were billions of people all around the world just like my now-dead family. I got up and looked out my window at the empty city. The buildings were all still there. The houses were all still there, for miles and miles and miles in every direction. And every one of those houses has photos just like this one. Photos of mothers and children, lovingly framed and crudely edited with magic markers... by people that weren't here anymore.

14

I felt overwhelmed.

I went back and picked up the cracked mirror from the floor. I could see myself... multiple versions of myself actually. Each piece of the cracked mirror showed a different angle for a different part of my face. An eye here, a cheek there. But the mirror didn't capture the whole me, only parts. I couldn't see *myself*, only individual aspects of myself. And those aspects didn't align. Who was I? I don't mean who did people think I was, but who was I, really? An eye? A cheek? A dutiful daughter? A quirky starlet? A fun piece of arm candy for a cute and successful older man? Could I be all of those things and none of those things? Were those things 'me' or were those things just faces that I put on in order to fit in, in order to be liked? I was an actress, comfortable and experienced in wearing someone else's skin as my own. But what did *my* skin look like? I searched deep inside, but found it hard to define myself in a way that wasn't related to how other people see me.

Now there were no more people. There was no more need to wear a mask. I let the mirror fall out of my hands and tumble onto the floor. I felt my mask falling away. But without a mask, did I have a face at all? Without other people, was I anything? A mirror is only a mirror when someone looks into it. Otherwise, it shows nothing.

Day 22:

I was sitting on the rocky riverbank. You had to climb over a fence to get here, but it wasn't that high. I had walked through this area hundreds of times over the years, but I never dared cross the three-foot high barrier down the embankment. I almost twisted an ankle on the fist-sized stones that made up the shore. Probably that was the reason there was a fence.

I picked up a rock and held it in my hand. It was warm from laying in the sun. It looked artificial, like it had been chipped from a bigger boulder somewhere and dumped here with all its friends, far from home. I threw it into the water. It made a plop.

"Elyse Morgan's gonna win an Emmy someday!" I shouted to the sky. I picked up another rock. "Elyse Morgan's gonna get an eight-figure movie deal!" The second rock plopped into the river next to its brother. "Elyse Morgan's the only person whose body is stupid enough to fight off the death virus!" Plop. "Elyse Morgan's gonna grow old and die alone and get eaten by rats or something 'cause there's no one left to bury her."

I started crying again. It suddenly welled up in me and when that happens, I can't stop it. I used to think it was a plus to be able to cry on cue. Now I just feel dehydrated. I reached into my bag and took out a plastic pill bottle. I dumped the contents into my hand. Six pills left.

"Elyse Morgan is gonna go crazy because there's no one left to refill her prescription..." I sobbed quietly.

Nearby, there is a bridge that crosses the river. It's pretty high up so the boats can go under. I silently started collecting up some of the rocks that lined the shore and stuffing as many as I could into the pockets of my jacket. I got up on my feet and climbed up the embankment, over the three-foot high fence, and down the road towards the end.

Soon, I found myself standing on the bridge, watching the water pass by below. I let a stone slip from my hand and then leaned over the railing to watch it fall. Tumble. Tumble. I could see the waves spread out in a rough circle, but it was too far to hear the plop. Gotta be high enough, right?

I put one leg over the railing, then the other. There was a tiny ledge to stand on. I grasped the railing tightly, so as not to slip prematurely. I remember breathing heavily. "1, 2, 3, easy as pie." I closed my eyes.

"Hey wait! Hey wait, you're alive!" someone said faintly. Was I hearing voices again? It had been weeks since I had spoken to another person. Was it a trick of the wind and the current? No. It was real. Someone, a mirage maybe, was running down the road towards me. I just froze, not knowing how to respond to this unexpected sight. He grabbed me from behind and started to hug. He held me from slipping off the ledge as my grip on the railing loosened. The first thing that struck me wasn't what he said, or what he looked like, but the warmth of his breath on the nape of my neck as his arms lifted me back over the railing. We stood eye to eye. His hands were on my cheeks and he pulled our faces together, closer, closer, until our foreheads were touching. "Hey... you're alive," he said softly, almost imperceptibly softly.

I was crying. Whether the tears had started before he arrived, or only after I saw his face, I don't know. "I don't want to be alive," I sobbed. "I don't want to be... anything. Everything is dead. I'm supposed to be dead."

He shook his head. "No, no, don't you get it?" he said with wonder and confusion on his face. "We're blessed. You are blessed, you are special. You are... you are supposed to be here. Out of all the billions of people in the world, you are still here. There's a reason for that. There's gotta be a reason for that. Everybody has somewhere they're supposed to be. I always thought that. And now all those people in that city they're... well, ok, they're supposed to be dead. But you, *you* are supposed to be alive. You and I are supposed to be alive. It's the only thing that makes sense." He paused and tried a half smile. There were tears welling up in his eyes. I didn't know what to say, so I said nothing.

"Okay. Okay, I see you're skeptical. But I can prove it to you." He took off his backpack and placed it on the ground. He sat down next to it with his legs crossed and unzipped the top. A ukulele appeared. He started singing. *Hey Jude. Don't be afraid. Take a sad song, make it better.* "See?" he said, putting the instrument back in the bag. "I always suspected I was destined to be the greatest singer on Earth. And now, despite not having a lick of talent, I am!" Okay, that was a dumb joke. And talking about it now, it doesn't sound like it was funny. But at the time, I just started laughing. Maybe it was just funny when compared to all the terrible things around us.

He saw me visibly relax. He knew I was safe now. He stood up and started dancing around in the goofiest way possible. He spoke in sing-song, "Hey pretty lady, can I buy you a drink? I've got a line of credit at the fanciest bar in town..." He reached out his hand and I took it. We walked together back across the bridge.

I sat with the stranger on a bench in front of a souvenir store that used to cater to the tourists that once walked up and down the riverbank. He didn't say all that much at first. He just stared at me in bewilderment; like he couldn't actually believe that I was sitting there in front of him. I guess I felt the same way. He told me his name, Benjamin. I dumped the rocks out of my jacket pocket into a pile on the sidewalk at our feet. We took turns standing up and throwing them into the river. You could hear each one splash as it struck the water.

He was talking. "So, it hit fast right? Did it hit you fast? I was driving home from work and the guy was talking on the news about people showing up at hospitals, and all of a sudden I felt like someone punched me in the stomach. I barely got home and into bed before I was down for the count. Did it hit you like that, too?"

I felt disadvantaged. Ben seemed to know a lot more about what happened than I did. "Actually, I don't even remember getting sick. I just woke up in bed and I felt like hell." I must have been one of the first ones to catch the sickness, before people started talking about it.

Ben continued to talk, like he didn't even hear my response. At the time, I guessed that he was just so excited to be talking to somebody... anybody... that all the words he'd been bottling up for the last month were just spilling out of him. "I wasn't even able to turn the television on when I was in bed. Whatever that bug was, it laid me out cold. One morning everything was fine and then the next morning... well, by then, the power was out."

It was hard for me to respond to him. I felt like I really didn't have anything valuable to add to the conversation. But I assumed at the time he wanted me to say something. "I don't even know how long I was sick. Maybe a day, maybe two? Long enough to be all gross and sticky." I threw another rock into the water. This one made a bigger ker-plunk than the others.

"Hey, did you do anything fun afterwards?" he said, his eyes brightening.

I was confused by the change of subject. "Fun?"

"Yeah, you know, *fun*?" He explained, "I mean it's the end of the world right? Everybody fantasizes about what they are going to do after the end of the world. You know what I did? The first thing I did? I mean after running around calling out to see if anyone else was still here, I mean."

I still didn't quite understand. "What?" What was fun about the end of the world?

He stood up, and started looking around for a rock to ker-plunk into the river. "I went to the bank. I had to smash the front window in with a brick, but I went to the bank. And I went into the vault and I dumped all the cash on the floor and I rolled around in it. Then I lit a cigar with a hundred-dollar bill." He paused for a second, picked up a stick, and tried to throw it. But it got caught in the wind and barely made it over the fence. It landed on the embankment. "I know, it's dumb, right? But that's what I did."

"I think I was too upset to fool around like that." My hands were in my pockets, and I remember squeezing my jacket tighter to hide my belly full of chocolate bars.

"It's a coping mechanism," he replied, trying to lighten the conversation. "If you don't laugh, you are just going to cry. And crying is how you end up on that bridge." I glanced up at the bridge, then downward in shame, saying nothing.

"Hey, I still have a whole wad of hundreds that I keep in my backpack to start fires." He smiled, awkwardly. "Seemed like an appropriate thing to do." He ran over to where I was standing and grabbed both of my wrists. "Oh my god, I just realized, can you believe we're the richest people in the world now?" He looked so hopeful; like a puppy that had just found his owner.

Our faces were just inches away from each other. I remember my lips involuntarily turning upward, in a melancholy smile. "Yeah, I suppose we are." Benjamin let go of my hands, reached into his pack, pulled out some crumpled bills and a lighter, and handed them to me.

"Go ahead. Try it!" I lit a handful of bills on fire. They burned brightly. I tossed them into the sky, where they dissolved into embers that blew away in the wind.

"Feels weirdly satisfying, right?" he said. I chuckled, reached into my pocket and threw one last, stray stone in the water. The weight I'd been carrying around for the last few weeks was lifting. I was so close to the end, and now? Now here, maybe, was a beginning.

"What did you do... Before... I mean, for a living?" he said, changing the subject once again. I remember very clearly that he told me, "I was a lawyer. Financial transactions, banking, stuff like that. It was okay I guess. Not as hard as you'd think. Had an office

21

big enough for a couch. Lucrative, too." He paused for a minute and glanced downward. "Not that it really matters anymore, I guess."

"I was an actress." It was weird having to actually say that to someone. Usually, the people I met were the sort of people who already knew. But he seemed genuinely surprised.

His eyes brightened. "Wow? Really? You made a living doing that? That's pretty intense. There's lots of people that say they are actresses, but usually they're mostly just waitresses."

As soon as he said that, he got this awkward look on his face, as if he'd said something insulting. But I wasn't insulted. It was kind of nice to talk about myself with someone who was honestly curious. Someone who didn't have an agenda, or want to use me for a connection. Benjamin seemed innocently interested. "Oh, I waited plenty of tables, too. Did some commercials here and there, but those don't pay enough to live on unless you get lucky. Then I got on a soap. The dialogue was terrible, but it was a job, you know?"

"Give me a sample?" he said, eagerly.

I did it way overdramatically, "Oh, Bradley, what am I going to do? My mother has threatened to cut off my trust fund if I don't agree to move back to the Hamptons. But I am and will always be... a Malibu girl!" I fanned myself with my hand and pretended to faint onto the bench as if I had the vapors.

Benjamin clapped overdramatically in response. "Bravo! I've never seen any soap operas. I don't even think my mom watched them when I was a kid. But I guess someone out there does... did." It's weird, thinking back. I guess everybody has the same blind spot; you and your circle assume what you do is so important to everybody, and one day you realize that, outside your circle, nobody cares a whit about you or the things you think are so important. I guess if the shoe was on the other foot, and I met some famous athlete, I'd have said the same thing about whatever sport he played. The Super Bowl is important to people who watch it, but I'd have no idea which teams were even playing.

"You'd be surprised how many times I'd get recognized. And how many creepers would send me things. Presents, flowers, naked drawings of themselves." I know it sounds like I'm being egotistical when I say that, but it's true. Not every day, but definitely sometimes.

"You had stalkers?" he said, "Wow."

"I don't know if I'd call them stalkers. Some of it got a bit creepy, but I never really felt I was in danger. It was just lonely losers living in their parents' basements with too much time on their hands." If anything, I felt kinda sorry for them.

"I guess you don't have to worry about that anymore, huh? No more naked drawings showing up in the mail." Ben realized too late that he'd brought up a reminder of how terrible things had become. My smile dissolved.

I turned away from him. "No, I guess not," I said wistfully.

"Wait a second," I heard him say. He ran around to get in front of me again, reached into his bag and pulled out some fresh strawberries. "Well, I don't have any flowers on me, and I can't draw a good rendition of my own butt, but here's a present you can have." I hadn't eaten anything fresh in a while. I took a strawberry and put it in my mouth. It was sweeter than

I remembered strawberries being. "Hey! You and I... we should do a team-up!" he said excitedly.

"A team-up?"

"Yeah. A team-up." He put another strawberry in my mouth. "Me and you. I don't know, maybe we are meant for each other or something." My mouth was too full to respond. "Look at you, you are beautiful. You might even have been in the running for most beautiful girl in the world before the plague. And you are definitely the most beautiful girl in the world now. And technically I'm the most handsome man in the world these days too. It's like a match made in heaven. We're both pretty lucky that we found each other, don't you think? Let's build on that."

I swallowed. "I don't know. I don't know you at all," I thought to myself. The berry was sweet, but still...

He was enthusiastic, at least I'd give him that much. "I'm not saying let's get married or anything. I'm not even saying that we should, like, start making out. Although, I mean you are super-hot. But I've got a place outside of town that I'm using as a home base. I've already stocked it with canned goods and a generator and stacks of hundred dollar bills to start fires with. It's got multiple bedrooms. You can come hang out with me for a bit and we could keep each other company and have somebody to talk to and set our broken legs in case we fall off a cliff." He waited for a response, but I didn't say anything. "At least until we find somebody else out here, I mean," he clarified.

I don't know, I don't know, I thought to myself. "My head is still so confused by all this. I'm not sure I'd really be an asset. I'd just slow you down." I was a wreck before all this happened, and I was tired. I didn't have a lot of fight left in me. Maybe it would be better if I just went back up on that bridge and...

"Hey. I'm safe," he said to me. His voice was strong and serious now. "Look me in the eye and you can see that." He grabbed my hands and looked down at my wrists. "Skin and bones. You're not eating properly. You were on that bridge because you figured you'd never be able to make it on your own. Tell me I'm wrong. You need someone in your life, everybody does. I do, that's for sure. And look around, who else is there? Neither of us have a lot of other options for company. You know?"

I looked down and there was still half a strawberry in my hand. I remember looking up at Benjamin and he was smiling hopefully. He was right, he felt "safe." He was goofy, and eccentric, and maybe he'd turn out to be an axe murderer. But that feeling of dread that had been knotted in my stomach was gone. For the first time since I woke up, I felt safe.

Day 29:

After that time on the bridge, the days passed by quickly. I remember it mostly as flashes, one experience jumping to the next. I guess that, without calendars or deadlines, every day was the same as the last, every hour was the same as the last. Maybe it had been a week since we met? In that time, I'm sure we went back to my apartment and packed up whatever of my life I'd decided I couldn't live without.

We were driving on a country road outside of town, through a deep forest. There was a house, warm and snug and isolated from all the reminders of death and decay around us. It was on a riverbank. The same river that the bridge crossed, probably. The house was clean and stocked with food and tins of hot cocoa.

We were standing on the covered porch that wrapped around the house, pointing at areas of the yard that could be used for a garden. Peas, tomatoes, kale, and sweet potatoes would grow nicely here, I thought. The porch had two rocking chairs on it. Ben told me they'd just been there when he found the house, but it seemed a sign that this place was meant to be shared by two people. By us.

We were sitting by a bonfire on the riverbank at sunset, drinking lukewarm beer. Ben was talking, but I don't remember the words. I remember laughing, and lying on my back with my arms straight out to my sides, wondering if a shooting star would pass overhead.

Day 38:

Another day. A week or two after the bonfire, I remember Ben suggesting a trip to the supermarket. It seemed healthy, normal. He made it seem normal. We weren't scrounging around for scraps in an abandoned ruin; we were consumers just doing what normal consumers did. Life felt like life felt before. Maybe even a little better than before, actually. I didn't have to worry about how I was going to pay for stuff. I didn't have to worry about people judging me for getting the fattening snacks. I didn't have to feel guilty for not giving a dollar to any kids collecting for their school trip. I didn't have to worry about being alone.

We pushed the cart through the aisles choosing canned goods for the week's dinners. Our footsteps and conversations echoed around the building. Ben picked up a phone and said, "Clean up on Aisle 8!" hoping the intercom still worked. It didn't. I laughed anyway. I remember taking some packets of seeds from the gardening section. I put some chocolate bars in my pocket for later.

There was a pharmacy at the back of the store. As we walked past it, I hesitated. Ben was far ahead. "C'mon," he shouted, "the cookies are this way." As he turned the corner, my face contorted into a look that might have been a half smile, or maybe a half-frown.

"Don't leave me behind!" I replied, hurrying to catch up.

Day 52:

We'd been at the cabin for a few weeks. Ben called it a 'cabin,' and I came to start calling it a cabin myself, but it wasn't a cabin at all. It was a pretty fancy house, tucked away on the shore of a river, miles outside of the city. The cabin was surrounded by woods, you couldn't even see it from the road. I don't know how Ben found it. He said a survivalist must have owned it. There was a generator and solar panels or whatever. It was warm and clean and dry and beautiful. The most beautiful house I ever lived in (sorry, mom).

It had a living room with one of those big vaulted ceilings, and the entire wall was made of windows. There was a big fireplace, and we snuggled on the couch in front of it every evening as we watched the sun set. Whoever owned the house had a bunch of wine, and we'd been going through it bottle by bottle, night by night. We played chess, and to his credit, I never felt that Ben was letting me win.

We were listening to jazz on a record player Ben found somewhere. He told me that the only way to "really" listen to jazz was on an old record player, filled with pops and scratches. There was almost always something playing in the background as we went about our daily business. "Without music, life would be a mistake," Ben told me once. Looking back, I think that maybe he was just afraid of silence.

During the days, we went about the chores of life. Neither of us had any idea what we were doing. But we figured it out. There was time. Ben was patient. That afternoon, I was sitting on the porch, drinking iced tea, watching him try to chop some firewood. Every time he balanced a log for chopping, the wind blew it over before he could pick up the axe. He must have reset it five times before he finally took a swing, and when he did, he completely missed the log. The axe went thud into the soil.

"Don't worry about messing up," I said, laughing hysterically, "We can always burn the evidence!"

Day 61:

Foraging is easier than you'd think. Just walk into the woods and pick berries. I would have thought life would be harder after the apocalypse. I would have thought things would be impossible. But they weren't. Everything was actually way easier. After only a few days with Ben at the cabin, I came to the realization that I didn't have to eat chocolate bars and stale cookies for the rest of my life. I could grow vegetables, and bake bread, and fix leaky pipes, and seal broken windows, and all those things that I would have called a repairman for, or gone to the store to buy, or just whined to mom about. Before all of this, before Ben, I could barely be bothered to learn how to brew coffee, and now, just like... two months later maybe, and I am walking out of the woods with a whole basket of fresh berries.

Sure, I was covered in dirt and mud and I ripped the hem of my pants, but I had berries fresher than I remember them ever being in the store. Even that organic market that everyone raved about.

The last time we went into town together, Ben and I looted a library for books we might need. I took a cookbook and hid it under my sweater so he wouldn't see. He still thought I didn't know how to cook.

Hours later, I was pulling a warm, gooey pie out of the oven.

And that was it, wasn't it? Meaning, purpose, happiness. Right there in a warm, gooey pie. Everything outside of this little shelter we built for ourselves was chaos, death, destruction, craziness, decay.

But not here in this little corner. Ben and I decided for ourselves to be happy.

We made this world for ourselves like we made this pie. We were making things right. Maybe not in terms of the whole world, but at least for us, at least in this one little garden of Eden we'd created, things were the way we wanted them to be, the way we made them be. Things were right.

Day 79:

For a while I'd been tracking the days and weeks on a calendar, figuring that sooner or later we'd meet up with other people, and I don't know, form a society I suppose? But on this day, I finally gave up. Ben never gave up. He kept saying that if the two of us were here, it stands to reason that there were probably other people around. Maybe not in this city, but surely in others.

I no longer cared. Society wasn't all that great. It was filled with petty people doing petty things. It was traffic jams, and waiting in line at the store, and whining about not being able to do things yourself. I didn't even miss my pills anymore. Was my anxiety from the chemicals in my brain, or from all those assholes I used to put up with every day? From my mom telling me to try harder, from my agent telling me to be prettier, from people I met in the street that wanted my photograph when all I wanted was to finish my fucking latte and get home.

It's so funny, me being here, like this, and somehow... *thriving*? Who would have thought? I'd been going through life with training wheels on. Scared to jump. But once I found myself without that safety net, I guess I found the strength to figure things out. Were other people inadvertently keeping me down by always being there for me? Weird way to think about things. The watchful gaze of everyone around me was meant to be comforting, meant to be helpful; but it was suffocating, and I didn't even realize how trapped I felt by it until being set free. I'd been passing judgment on myself based on how I appeared to others. Without that watchful eye, I was free to not be who I was expected to be. Free to take a risk and not worry about other people saying, "We told you so." If I messed something up, I'd just sweep up the broken parts and try again.

That afternoon, we were sitting on the front porch of the cabin, because the sun was out and it was warm. I was learning to cut hair. I knew I was going to make a mess of it. "But," I told Ben, "I'm the only one who has to look at you, so really, if I mess up, I'm only hurting myself." He didn't complain. Unlike most people I'd known previously, he complained only rarely.

Day 97:

I remember tending to seedlings in the garden. The garden was more than just a way to get fresh vegetables. It was a sort of hope for the future, I guess. After all, no one plants a garden without the optimism of being around to pick the fruit. Working on the garden was my way of reminding myself that I was going to be around for a while.

I remember being on my hands and knees, looking at the small plants growing out of the ground. I remember the smell; grassy... planty... whatever you call it. I remember chickens scratching in the dirt nearby. This is all real. I know that this is all real. Knew that this was all real. That's important for later.

A car was approaching. Ben had returned. I didn't get up right away. I was still digging out weeds. The sound of a car door. He was halfway down the drive by the time I rose and met him. He was carrying two big, canvas bags. I remember I was smiling.

"Well, the only artichokes I found were expired, and one of the cans on the shelf was blown out, so I decided to skip those," he said as I took one of the bags from him. "But the capers still looked good, so I grabbed a few jars. We can make a Puttanesca." I looked at him blankly, "Puttanessca has capers in it, right?" he added sheepishly.

"Sort of." I was becoming proud of my newfound ability to cook. Or at least the newfound ability to read cookbooks now that I had infinite time on my hands. "I can make do, assuming we can sub some basil for the garlic."

He glanced over at the makeshift garden I had been tending. "Are the cucumbers ready yet? I picked up a bottle of ranch dressing!" He reached into the bag and pulled out a bottle. He shook it to see if it had gone bad. "Hmm, well maybe it's now blue cheese dressing. That's still probably edible, right?"

"I just put the cucumbers in last week. They're barely sprouts. You won't have cucumbers for a month or two at least." I poked at his jeans playfully. "I'm the only one who gets a cucumber around here these days." I remember winking playfully.

Ben put his free arm around me as we walked towards the cabin. "Yeah, baby. I knew there was a reason I keep coming back here."

"I've told you a thousand times now, I'm only dating you because you are literally the last man on earth." I said as overdramatically as possible.

"Really? I'm crushed." He turned away from me and pretended to sulk. I stopped, put the bag down, and put my hand on his shoulder. He turned and faced me and I looked at him directly, eye to eye.

"You know I'm joking," I said. "Out of all the people I could've spent the apocalypse with, I got lucky. You're resourceful, and caring, and patient. And you're sooooo nice. It's a refreshing upgrade from the self-absorbed losers I used to date." He smiled. I remember him smiling. It was an authentic smile. "I'm enjoying being with you so much, and weirdly, I don't think it's just because it's the end of the world. You really are a great guy. It's funny, you know, I probably never would've given you a chance before all this, but in a strange way, I'm kinda glad it happened."

We continued down the stone path through the garden and up the stairs to the porch of the cabin. I placed the bag on the floor, gave Ben a light kiss on the cheek, and returned to my gardening. Ben sat on the steps and watched me. "Well, I hope you'll continue to feel the same way about me when we finally find someone else still alive," he said as he opened a pack of stale cookies he'd pulled from one of the bags.

"Of course, dummy. I'm *digging* you." I held up my trowel for comedic effect. "The introduction of some new people into our world isn't going to change that." I didn't understand why he felt insecure. "You're probably right in that maybe, if there'd been a bunch of hot dudes around when we met, you'd have to fend off the competition from the other villagers, but I'm yours now. All yours."

"Thanks," he replied, reassured. "You know, I feel really lucky, too. I never really dated much before the world ended. And certainly nobody in your league, which is way out of my league."

"I do have an amazing booty, I agree," I gave him a wiggle.

"It's not just the amazing booty. You're really cool, and you were like, famous and stuff. Plus, you are infinitely nicer than someone as hot as you should be."

It was... different... to have someone compliment me on my niceness. People usually complimented me on other things. They'd say how pretty I was, or how famous I was, or how good I was at something they wish they were good at themselves. Ben didn't know me from before, when I was popular and always hiding behind a shield to stop people from trying to use me. Ben didn't use me. He didn't ask anything of me. He just wanted my company, and he wanted it because of *me*, because of who I was, not how it would improve his status or to show me off as some kind of trophy.

"Meh. I wasn't always so nice," I responded. "There were always creepers around. So many creepers. Not just meatheads in bars and catcallers in the street. Even the other actors were creepers. And the directors... and the casting agents... and the musicians... and the creepy millionaires."

"Millionaires?"

"Oh yeah. You have no idea. You get booked on a television show, or even a commercial, and all of a sudden your agent starts getting calls from rich old dudes asking to take you out to dinner to 'talk about a project.' Ick." It was totally true. I could tell you all sorts of tales about people you've definitely heard of.

"Well, as it just so happens, I'm a millionaire now." Ben said.

"Oh really?" I leaned against my shovel and pretended I didn't believe him.

"Yup," he said, play-acting like he wanted to impress me. "Remember when I told you I went to a bank and threw all the money on the floor and rolled around in it? Afterwards I claimed it as all mine. In fact, I'm probably, like, a billionaire. So deal with it."

"Ooooh," I swooned. "I've never dated a billionaire before. I hope all that money doesn't change you." I laughed.

He got up and pranced around, "Too late. I'm a fancy-lad now," he said with a mock posh accent. "Stick with me, baby. I'll give you that gold-plated yacht you've always dreamed of." He pretended to sip from a teacup with his pinky pointed outward.

He reached into one of the bags he retrieved from town. A small, white, cardboard box appeared. "Speaking of gifts, here's those pills you ordered." He tossed the box toward me. It was the prescription anti-psychotic pills I'd asked for. I don't remember exactly when I opened up to Ben about my past, but it was definitely sometime before then. It was hard talking about things. Well, I mean that... with most people it was hard talking about things. With Ben, for the first time, maybe, I didn't feel like I needed to hide things about who I was. About what I'd been through. About what I needed to stay functional. "I got the freshest ones they had, but they expired a few weeks ago," he said. "I hope they are still good."

"I'm sure they'll be fine. I'm in a much better place mentally, anyway. There's so little stress here. Everything is easy and quiet and perfect." Those days, the pills were really more of a precaution than anything else. There were no voices here at the cabin. Just the wind and the river and sometimes a bird calling from the trees.

Ben jumped down off the step and came over to the garden. "Oh, and here's another special delivery just for you." He was holding a small basket of fresh strawberries. "Picked fresh today."

"Oooh. My favorite! How'd you know?" I said, mouth full of berry. I definitely remember a drop of juice on my chin. I finished chewing. A glint in my eye. "Well, my second favorite...," I said suggestively.

"Second favorite? My sources have misinformed me! I could've sworn it was strawberries. What pray tell is your favorite then?"

"Cucumbers..."

"Oh, my!" He exclaimed in mock embarrassment. I smiled seductively. He moved closer and put his arm around me. "I suppose I know where I might be able to find one of those," he said suggestively. "Follow me, my dear."

I let the shovel fall behind me as we headed out of the garden, up the steps, and into the cabin.

Day 100:

It was on the hundredth day that everything collapsed.

It wasn't the same day that I just spoke about, it was definitely a different day. But it was similar to that day. I was sitting at the picnic table in the yard near the garden, sorting seedlings. This time Ben wasn't arriving, he was leaving. Leaving to go explore the city. Leaving to find food and things for us to play with, and music for us to listen to. And maybe people. He always held out hope of people being out there.

I watched him walk to the car. He opened the door, waved, and got in. I could hear the car's engine fade into the distance as he got further and further away from me. He'd be back in a few hours. He was always back in a few hours. I never remembered him being gone for more than a few hours.

I just stared off into space for a bit after he left. Listening to the wind as it rushed through the trees. Looking at the plants and the water and the cabin and the life we'd built. I never went into the city with Ben in those days. I could never bring myself to go into the city with Ben. That's where the reminders were. Reminders of my previous life, reminders of what happened. Reminders of death and destruction. Triggers. You may think me weak, but it was better here. So much better. So much easier to just stay at this pleasant little house in the woods and pretend the rest of the world didn't exist. Pretend that none of those people from my past ever existed. Pretend that none of those people were lying dead in the streets or in their beds silently rotting away with no one left to bury them.

No. Stop thinking about that.

I got up and went back to the garden. The weeds weren't going to pick themselves. I was covered in dirt. I remember that I heard a rustle coming from the woods, although it was certainly nothing. I don't know why I remember that. I went back to my seedlings. That noise again, it wasn't a rustle, it was something different. Natural and unnatural at the same time; like maybe a rustle that someone had once recorded and was now playing back in reverse. I felt a presence, the chill shiver of a ghost floating by. I looked behind me.

Standing there, plain as day, was Hector. Were my eyes deceiving me? Hector! If there was one person I wished to see in this world again it was Hector! Hector in his oversized baggy sweater that he always wore. Hector with his hair tussled and in desperate need of a comb. I realize haven't explained who Hector is just yet.

"Hector?"

"Hey sis," he said as nonchalantly as if he'd just come from the other room. As if he'd always expected to see me again. He waved, sheepishly. I dropped my shovel and ran over to where he was standing at the edge of the garden.

The words spilled out of my mouth. "Oh my god! Hector? You are alive? Where have you been?" I had so many questions. "I'd hug you but I'm filthy! I can't believe you are here! I thought I was the only one. I mean, I thought we were the only ones. You have to

41

meet Ben. He's here. I mean he's not *here* here, he drove off to town to get supplies. I told him we didn't need anything, but he goes off every day. I think it's because he is looking for other survivors, but he won't say that, he doesn't want to get my hopes up I guess. It's been months. But you are a survivor, you are here. It's crazy, right?"

"Is that really you?" he responded, almost without emotion. He squinted, as if he were trying to spot me from far away.

"What do you mean, 'is it me?' Who else would it be?" It had been months, and I guessed that maybe he couldn't believe his eyes. I mean, I recognized him right away, but still, it was so weird, so improbable, that he would just walk out of the woods like that. I assumed he must have been as stunned as I was.

"I mean, is it really *you* you, not some A.I.?" he said. "You're not another fake you, are you?"

"You aren't making any sense." I took a step backwards. I wasn't frightened. I'm sure I wasn't frightened. But I was... confused maybe? There was something wrong. For the first time in weeks I felt that there was something wrong.

"No... No, I suppose I'm not," he said. He bit his lip and turned away from me. He took a few steps, like he was trying to gather his thoughts. "I'm sorry. It's just... there's been so many dead ends." He rubbed his hands over his forehead. "I've been searching for you for a long time now, and I'm finally getting close."

How was he not giddy like I was? Had he been hurt, or lost his mind from loneliness? No, that wasn't what losing one's mind was like. "Getting close?!? You're here, you found me!"

He suddenly jerked his head off to the side, as if he was hearing a voice. "Okay... Okay...," he said, responding to something I couldn't hear.

"Hector?"

He turned back to face me, our gazes locked on each other's eyes. "Elyse, where are you?"

"I'm right here, in front of you." I smiled a half smile. I remember that I was starting to notice that there was a disconnection between Hector and the rest of the world. Like when you look at a photo and you can tell that someone has been edited in. Something subtle about the shadows or something. You can't put your finger on why you know they aren't supposed to be in the photo, but you just know.

"I mean, where do you *think* you are?" he replied. I remember he looked more than anything else... concerned. I'd seen that look before. Back in the dark days. Back when I was having problems and everybody was treating me with kid gloves and tiptoeing around me. Never wanting to say anything or do anything that might make me react badly. I didn't like that look. I hated that look. That look brought back bad memories. Hector was bringing back bad memories. I stared at him blankly.

"You don't know, do you?" he said, seemingly as much to himself as to me. "Of course. Why would you?" He smiled, a more natural smile than last time. "Listen to me. I don't have much time. Your life here. Doesn't something seem a bit... wrong?"

"A bit wrong?"

"Like, something is not quite right with this world." He looked around; at the trees, at the clouds in the sky, at the water rushing by in the river, at the tomato plants that were now just starting to sprout

43

small, green fruit. I looked around too, there wasn't anything wrong with this little world... I mean this little life Ben and I had made.

"Well, everybody's dead," I joked. Half-joked.

"Isn't that a bit too convenient? What made you so special to survive? I mean you in particular. Somehow billions of people don't make it, and you do. You aren't suspicious?"

"You survived, too. Maybe it's genetic, do you think it could be something genetic..."

He cut me off, he was talking faster now. "...and somehow, despite all those odds, you ended up here; happy, warm, well-fed, in domestic bliss. Not a care in the world. Nothing scary or distressful. Every comfort delivered right to your front door each afternoon."

We were talking over each other. "I knew you'd come back. I knew it. I didn't want to believe it..." I started to lose it. My stress level can only get so high before I start to freak out. I could feel that knot in my stomach. A full on panic attack was coming. And it was radiating from Hector. Hector was the cause; what he was saying, how he was acting. Hector never acted like that in the past. He always knew how to calm me down when I started to freak out. He was always gentle with me. He wasn't acting like the Hector I remembered.

"Elsie, things aren't what they seem. You're in danger."

"Unless..."

"I don't know how long I can keep this connection open."

I started just talking to myself. "I'm sure Ben would have noticed if I was acting crazy. He'd have said something. I've been on meds. I know what's real and what's not real," I was saying.

"Listen to me," Hector said.

"How did you survive the apocalypse?" I asked him.

"Listen to me!" he shouted, trying get me to focus.

"How did you survive the apocalypse?!?!" I screamed hysterically. There were tears streaming down my cheeks.

"Goddamnit, there was no apocalypse," he shouted at me. "Ever. It's all still there."

That didn't make any sense at all. "It's not. It's not still there. Have you been to the city? There's no one there. I've was stuck the city for weeks and there is no one left. There's not one person. No one but me and Ben. That's it. Me and Ben. And you, but you came out of nowhere. You can't be here." Nothing made sense at all. Everything had made sense that morning, everything made sense in the garden with the plants and hearing Ben's car drive off and watching the river and the clouds, and now nothing made sense anymore.

"I'm not here. This is not an actual place."

I started to come to a realization. "Of course... you *can't* be here. It doesn't make sense. I'm just imagining things again." I started to bang the sides of my head with my fists.

"I *am* here," Hector said calmly. "I'm here and I'm not here. It's complicated."

"I'm just imagining things again, like I used to," I mumbled to myself.

"You aren't imagining things," he replied.

I was mad now. Mad at him, mad at myself. Mad at my stupid broken brain that made stuff up. "I *am* imagining things. You are here, you aren't here. You can't be here. But here you are." One of my psychiatrists once told me that the world made sense, and when things didn't make sense, when something was happening that couldn't be happening, or that didn't fit with how I knew the world worked, that was a sign it was just a hallucination. Reality has to make sense, hallucinations don't.

"What do you know about this Benjamin person? What has he told you?" Why was Hector asking me about Ben?

"Ben? He's just this guy." I said those words, but Ben was more than just 'a guy.' "He found me in the ruins. I was alone and he found me. He saved me. He stopped me from jumping off a bridge." Without him....

"What did he tell you about himself? Who did he say he was?" Hector was questioning me like he would interrogating a criminal.

"He said he was a lawyer or something. What difference does that matter now? There isn't anything left. Hector, why are you doing this to me?"

Hector sighed. From the look on his face I could tell he realized that he was doing more harm than good. He calmed his voice. "He's not a lawyer Elyse. He's a computer scientist. A good one. What has he told you about computers?"

"Computers?" That came out of nowhere. "Nothing. He hasn't said anything about computers." I was puzzled. How would Hector even know anything about Ben? They'd never met. I mean, I assume they'd never met. When would they have met? From before somewhere?

Hector continued, getting aggressive again. "Has he mentioned anything about a secret place he has? Maybe just let something slip that seemed weird. A cabin, a storage locker, something like that?"

"What is going on? What is happening to me? Hector! Are you real? Is this real?" I was panicked. Not because of the questions, or not because of how Hector was yelling at me, but because all of a sudden, things didn't make sense. And when things didn't make sense, that meant that my stupid brain was doing stupid brain stuff again. And that could get bad. It had been bad. Really bad. And they always told me, "Elyse, you need to stay on your meds or else you'll relapse." And I did. I did stay on my meds. And things weren't bad. Things were good. Even when the world ended, things weren't bad. And now all of a sudden they were bad again, and there weren't any doctors I could go to, or friends or family that would be there to talk me through it. Just Ben, just Hector maybe? Or was he the delusion? I remember my mind racing a mile a minute. Hector was still talking I think, but I couldn't make out what he was saying.

"Elyse, focus." Hector said sternly. He snapped his fingers in my face. "None of this is real. This house, the apocalypse, these tomatoes you are growing. Those trees. It's not real."

"It's not real?"

"What do you remember just before you woke up here, before everyone died and the world ended?" Hector said.

"I was in my apartment. I was... I was..."

47

"You've been kidnapped, Elyse. I've been looking for you for weeks now. We've all been looking for you. This Benjamin guy, he's not some guy who found you in the ruins. He's a stalker. He saw you on television and he stalked you and he kidnapped you. And he put you in his machine."

"Machine? What machine?" There were no more machines.

"This," Hector cried, waving his hands about. "This machine. This simulation. This virtual reality. It's not real. None of this is real. The world didn't end. It's all still here. Your friends, your family, the police, we're all still out here looking for you. You are strapped into a machine. This Benjamin guy didn't save you. He trapped you."

"No. No, no, no... He saved me. When no one else was there for me, he saved me." You can recognize delusions, they told me, because delusions don't fit in. You can recognize *paranoid* delusions when things that don't fit in try to turn you against your support system. Ben was my only support... of course a delusion would try to get me to doubt him.

But... Hector was not a delusion. Hector was serious. Hector made sense. Even as he didn't make sense, he made sense. "...this guy calling himself Ben was part of a team of engineers working on a new kind of virtual reality game." Hector was talking, Hector was explaining. "Very advanced, very immersive. Once you are hooked up, you can't even tell you are in it. But he saw you on television, and he wanted you. He figured you wouldn't date him unless he was the last man on earth. So, that's what he did. He made himself literally the last man on earth. He trapped you inside his machine and he hid the machine away. He leaves you

48

there day and night. And when he wants to play with you, he logs on and joins in. But none of this is real."

"No no no no no no no." I ran from Hector. He followed, trying to reason with me. "This isn't some video game." I cried. "This doesn't look like a video game. It's real." I picked a tomato from the garden. I remember holding it up in front of him. I may have even taken a bite. "This is real, it feels real, it tastes real." The tomato was unripe and bitter.

Hector's voice was stern and serious and in a way comforting. Even if what he was saying was crazy. "This isn't an ordinary video game. Things here aren't made up of pixels and bytes. The interface works directly with your brain. It's more like... more like a dream. There isn't a data file drawing an image of a tomato, it's like it just tells your brain that you are holding a tomato and your brain and your memory just does the rest. That tomato looks and feels the way your mind assumes a tomato looks and feels."

I threw the tomato to the ground and ran into the house. "No. It's real. This is all real. I'm not crazy!" I shouted. I ran around, picking up objects. "This plate is real." I threw the plate onto the floor. It shattered. "This mug is real." The mug shattered too. "This table is real." I banged on its surface with my hands. It was hard and solid and made of dark wood. It smelled of polish. I hit it and hit it and hit it until my hands hurt. I looked up, and Hector was standing in the doorway. Just standing, his face in shadow from the sun streaming in behind him.

I picked up one of the records Ben had brought from town, and showed it to him. "Look at this." I challenged him. "A Bud Powell record. I never heard of this guy. My mind can't just make up a jazz record I've never heard of, right? Where did this come from?"

"I know it seems real," Hector said calmly, "But in your heart, you know that this place is just a dream.

"You think I'd dream of this?" I threw the record at him like a Frisbee. He didn't even flinch as it sailed past his head.

"It's not your dream. It's *his* dream. Is this the life you want? Is this the life you think you deserve? You don't belong here." Was that my self-doubt talking? Was he right? This fantasy garden of Eden. Bliss and freedom from pain and suffering and all the crazy of society. Is that 'me'? Or is 'me' the person who struggles and juggles a dozen friendships with fake people, and doesn't have a boyfriend because every man I meet is a creeper, and I'm fighting tooth and nail to keep my job in the industry. Fighting tooth and nail to stay sane and out of the mental hospital and I'm a bad daughter and a bad sister and a bad girlfriend and a bad actress, and a bad roommate and I swear too much and drink too much and eat too much candy and....

I slumped into a chair. "Where do I belong then?" Defeated.

"You belong at home. With us. With your life and your friends and your career."

"But that doesn't exist!" Hector was right, I didn't belong here, but the place I belonged to wasn't a thing anymore. I could no more go back to my old life than I could resurrect someone from the dead. Resurrect Hector from the dead.

Hector came and kneeled down beside me. He put his hands on the armrest of the chair I'd flopped into. He leaned in. "Calm down, you have to listen to me. It does exist. We can get you out of here. We can still save you."

Delusions will destroy you, my psychiatrist said. Unless you recognize them and challenge them. "It doesn't exist. Ben says I have to accept that it's all gone."

"It does. I'm proof of that. Ben doesn't have your interests at heart." He seemed so sincere. I remember how sincere he sounded. I put my head in my hands and rocked back and forth.

"No no no no no. He wouldn't do that." Ben was a good guy. I'd been sure that Ben was a good guy. Was he the bad guy now? Wait, was I the bad guy now? If I don't belong here, then where do I belong? Is this the fantasy world? I remember coming to the realization that maybe Hector wasn't the hallucination, maybe Hector wasn't the delusion. Maybe Hector was the one thing that was real, it was everything else that was the delusion. Had I fallen so far? I wasn't just hearing voices like last time, I was now hearing an entire universe?

Hector was definitely right when he said that this world didn't make sense. What were the chances of just me and Ben being the only two people in the world to survive? And then to find each other? It was absurd. And okay, even if we just got really, really lucky, what was the point of all of this? What was the point of life in this empty place? I'd been happy, I suppose. Each separate minute, each separate hour, was pleasant. But what was the point? There was no point in living here in this empty world, just waiting 'til when? When we grow old and die and that's the end of human civilization? Seems pointless. And even if we ended up having some kids, we'd just doom them to live pointless lives here among the ruins too. No, there was no *purpose* here. But if the real world existed out there somewhere, maybe that's where purpose was? Maybe that's where everything might make sense again? Wasn't it worth it to believe in what Hector was telling me? Maybe it wasn't real, but what if it was? Wasn't it worth it to at least try to get back there?

"I'm sorry," Hector said.

I didn't want to live in this fantasy anymore. I wanted everything to be the way it was. The way it was supposed to be. The way I deserved it to be. "I don't know what to do. I'm trapped here. I can't see the exit." It'd been months since I fell into this fantasy. I didn't know if Hector was telling the truth about some computer thing, or if I'd just had a complete psychotic break, but what he'd told me had suddenly poisoned everything. I didn't want to be here anymore.

"This isn't the real world, you see that now? Thank God." Hector replied. "The good news is that we can bring you back to the real world. The world where everything is still here, everybody is still here. It's all waiting for you; your friends, your apartment, your job, that coffee shop down the street that makes those overpriced lattes you can't stop drinking."

"Why haven't you saved me? Hector, you have to save me!" I pleaded.

"It's all there, we can bring you back. But you have to help us, you have to believe in me."

"How can I do anything from in here?" I couldn't breathe. I felt like I was suffocating. There was no air here. It was all fake air, computer air. If the wind wasn't real, how could the oxygen be?

"We don't know exactly where you are. He's hidden your body away somewhere. We just need to know where you are and the police can come get you, come free you. Benjamin is using some distributed net mainframe or something, and we've hacked into that, but that's not enough. It's like if you are chatting with someone on the phone. You can talk to them, but you don't know where in the world they are exactly. I can talk to you, but I don't know where you are."

"Where am I? Where did he put me?!?" It's an odd feeling not knowing where you are. Am I in a dissociative state again?

Hector continued, "He had to have put you somewhere safe. We think he strapped you into a chair or something and put you in a warehouse, or a basement, or a storage room, or something like that. You've just got to find out where exactly that is. Has he ever said anything? Talked about a place somewhere? Maybe in another city, a place where he keeps stuff?" I didn't remember Ben ever saying anything like that. He didn't like to talk much about the past. Who could blame him? I didn't either. I wasn't really sure about anything about Ben's life; where he was from, what his childhood was like, who he used to date. I guess I figured it didn't matter. But talking to Hector like this made me question Ben's motives. Was it just avoidance or painful memories, or something more sinister? "Maybe he let something slip," Hector continued. "Think, you have to think. He must have said something."

"I... I don't know." It was hard to remember everything he might have said over the past few months.

"Okay. Well then, you'll have to trick him into saying something. Ask him about his past, don't tip him off, but ask him about himself. Listen. Listen close. Get me an address, get me a clue, get me anything, and

I'll come for you, I promise. Have faith in me. Just get me some leads. Can you do that?" I didn't answer at first. "Can you do that?" he said again.

"I think so. I don't know. I think so."

Hector's face said to me, 'that's all she's capable of, it'll have to do for now.' He nodded slightly and said, "I'll be close. I'm going to go before he gets back. He can't know anything's changed. That would be bad. He's unstable. We don't know what he'll do if he's threatened. Be careful, don't let him know you are suspicious. I'll check in on you again as soon as I can."

A car engine could be heard outside. Ben was back from wherever it was he'd been. I turned towards the window. I could still hear Hector speaking, but I remember it sounded far away, like he was speaking from deep inside a tunnel. "Good luck, Elyse," he said. "Stay strong. We're all waiting for you right here on the other side. We haven't forgotten about you."

I ran to the window to see Ben getting out of the car. I turned around, but Hector was no longer there.

Still Day 100:

Was Hector real? No, he definitely wasn't real. Not *real* real. But was he fake real? I'm not making any sense. I mean, I was trying to decide if Hector was who he said he was; an angel sent from the world outside of this one where everything was still alive and bright, or if he was just a misfiring of my dumb brain, confusing me like my dumb brain often did. I don't remember Ben coming into the house, but there was his voice in the doorway. He was carrying a large bag. "Hey, baby girl!" he said, as if nothing was wrong. As if nothing was different. As if everything hadn't just collapsed. But I guess that of course he would act as if nothing was wrong.

I remember just standing by the window, not responding. Just staring at him. Was Ben real? Was he *real* real, or just fake real like maybe Hector was. He just barged in and set his bag on the table. He rambled, seemingly oblivious to everything I'd just experienced, "So, I didn't find any super-interesting new foods to try, but I remembered there's that old record store downtown. Did you ever go in there? I never did, back before. But I went in there today and grabbed a whole pile of some classy jazz albums. I'll play one tonight at dinner. I still have some candles left and we've got wine and...," he trailed off. By now he could tell that something was wrong. "You okay, babe?" he asked with a half-smile.

"Where did you say you lived? Before all this?" I said it bluntly. Too bluntly, I'm sure. Keep it under control, Elyse. Acting. You can do this.

"Over in the hills on the north part of town. I had a dreary apartment on a side street not too far from that park with the ridiculous modern art sculpture in the middle, I told you that."

"Can we go there? To your old apartment?"

"Um. I suppose we could go someday. But there isn't anything worth going back there to see. I took all the stuff I cared about with me and brought it here." Was he suspicious, confused, bored, evasive? Hard to tell.

"I just want to know about you. I want to know about your old life. I want to see your office."

"My office?" Ben seemed surprised.

"Yeah. You had an office, right? Everybody with a job had an office. The building didn't collapse, did it? Or fall into a pit that opened in the surface of the earth? It's still there, right? Why can't we go look at it?"

"Yeah. Yeah, of course we can go look at it. Anytime." He smiled and tried to brush of his earlier reluctance. "I suppose that it's like, what's the point? That life doesn't exist anymore. I'm kind of a new person, just like you are a new person. The past doesn't matter so much. I'm just worried that it'll dredge up sad memories." He paused for a second, "But sure. Let's make plans to go in a few days, ok?"

"I want to see all your old haunts," I said with as realistic a smile as I could muster. "I want to see the bars you used to go to and the hole-in-the-wall restaurant that you thought had the best burrito in the city, and the musty little shop in an alley where you bought all those books you claim you've read. I want to dig into that storage place you rented and thumb through old cardboard boxes of your childhood

56

memorabilia. I want to see all of it. We're together now, you should show me everything." I finished with, "No secrets, right?"

He nodded. "Sure. Sure, we can do that, baby. Make a whole day of it. I don't think I ever said anything about a storage place though. Where'd you get that idea?"

"I don't know. Just assumed. Maybe someone told me in a dream." I remember trying to laugh, but I don't think it came off as authentic.

Ben closed in and put his hands on my shoulders. There was a look of concern in his eye. Or maybe it was suspicion. Or maybe I'm not remembering things right at all. "Are you okay, baby? You don't seem like you are doing okay."

I remember my façade suddenly falling away, like a cracked porcelain mask flaking off to reveal my true face. "I don't know Ben. You tell me? Do I look okay? Why don't you figure out what's wrong with me on your computer?" It sounded flippant and sarcastic. I'm sorry Hector, I just can't pretend when I'm upset and anxious.

"A computer? I don't think computers work anymore honey. Not for stuff like that. There's no internet left."

"Well, fix it then," I snapped at him. "You're a computer genius. Can't you just fix it? That seems to be what you are best at, fixing things. Fixing problems. Fixing me."

"Computer genius?" he replied, maybe, just maybe, with a hint of nervousness in his voice. "What are you talking about? I don't know anything at all about computers."

"Oh no? Then how did I get here?" I shouted. "Why would Hector say all those things to me?" The first tears fell.

"Hector? Your brother? Elyse, sweetie, Hector died a long time ago."

"No, he didn't, Ben! He was right here. I was just talking to him. He was right here...." I spun around, but Hector was gone. Had he been here at all? Yes, he was just here. Even though he wasn't *here* here, I knew in my heart that he was still here. Had been here. "He was telling me things, things about you. About your lies. This isn't real, Ben. None of this is real. I knew in my heart something was wrong, but it's not *something* that's wrong, it's *everything* that's wrong."

"Elyse, calm down. You say you talked to your brother? Were you hallucinating?"

"It wasn't a hallucination!" I shouted. Then my volume decreased to almost a whisper. "He was right here, right in front of me. We were talking." I remember realizing that I sounded crazy. I looked around, but there was no trace of Hector anywhere.

"Elyse, if he was right here, where did he go?"

"He... he just disappeared. He wasn't really here, I mean... he wasn't *here* here. He was outside. He was outside this world, in the real world. He wanted me to go to him."

"Outside? Like in the garden?" He turned and craned his neck to look out the big, bay window.

"Yes, the garden... But no, that's not what I meant. I meant he was outside of this *world*, looking in... from the real world, the one that counts." I imagined being caught in a snow globe and looking up into the sky and seeing Hector's face looking down on me, all distorted from the dome of glass that separated us.

"You aren't making any sense." I could tell I was stressing Ben out. Unlike my family, he wasn't used to me acting like this. He wouldn't possibly know what to say to talk me down off the ledge. Not like Hector does. Not like Hector did. I ran back out onto the porch. The world, the garden, the sky, the river, it was starting to look real again. I stood there confused and panting, as if I'd just woken up from a terrible dream.

Ben cautiously came outside and stood behind me silently, waiting for me to calm down. "Nothing makes sense," I said, hesitantly. "Nothing has made sense for months. I'm not supposed to be here. I'm not supposed to be in this place. Nothing we do here matters. It's not real."

He put his hand on my shoulder. "Baby. Stay with me. You have to stay with me. You have to understand— this is real. I don't want it to be real any more than you do, but this is real." He stepped down into the yard and picked up a fistful of the freshly turned soil. He let it fall to the ground through his fingers. "This is what's left, we're all that's left. Do you understand?" I stood silently as Ben wiped his hand on his shirt, leaving a stain. I was worried that he'd gotten his shirt all dirty because of me. Weird, right? His face had that half-smile he gets when he was thinking hard. "Maybe it's your meds. Remember how you said you used to have delusions?"

"That was a long time ago. I'm better now."

"The delusions went away because you were taking your meds. But all the meds in the world are expired now. There's no one to make fresh pills." He paused for a second. "Maybe we've got to up the dose or something, I don't know. I'm not a doctor. But you understand that you have hallucinations, right?" I slumped down and sat on the step. Ben sat down next to me and held me tightly. We rocked back and forth for a while. "That's all Hector was, another hallucination." Ben whispered softly in my ear. "You just had an episode. I know you are sad. I know you feel guilty because all your friends are dead and you lived. I know you think everything is meaningless. I know that you feel lonely because there's no one to talk to except the chickens and me, and I'm just some doofus who is probably the last person in the world you wanted to spend the rest of your life with. But you need to stay strong. You can't survive if you don't stay strong. I can't survive here without you. You are my rock. I need you to be my rock. Now come inside, I found some wild scallions, I was going to make some sort of stir fry with them. We'll eat some rice, open a bottle of wine. Get to bed early. I'll go scrounge around for some medical books tomorrow, see if I can't figure something out."

He stood and lifted me up onto my feet. I remember being really tired all of a sudden. That always happened after an episode. Drained. As we went back inside I could hear Ben saying to me, "In the meantime, you've got to stay with me, okay? You have to understand that even if you see something weird, it's not real. It's just an illusion. You and me, we're the only real people here. Keep repeating that to yourself."

Day 103:

I didn't sleep much that night, or the next, or the next, I think. I remember lying awake in bed. I guess there must have been a full moon because it was just light enough to see the shadows of the things we kept by the bedside. Some books, a wind-up alarm clock, a pile of clothes covering a chair. It wasn't light enough to really make them out clearly; you could only discern their outlines. Is a closed book in a dark room, unreadable, still a book?

Ben was lying on his side, turned away from me. I was on my back staring up at the ceiling. I could hear him breathing softly. Could feel the rhythm of his body as he inhaled and exhaled. I could hear the rustling of the trees outside. The window was open. A fresh breeze flowed through the room. Everything looked real. Was this a dream? In dreams aren't there some things you aren't supposed to be able to do? I remember hearing that. Like read a book or something maybe? I tried pinching my arm, but my arm felt real. I didn't wake up.

It was so quiet here. When I was a kid, the house was crowded. People tried to be quiet, of course, but even after my bedtime, I could hear my parents talking in the kitchen, or my older brother banging around, or the hum of the dishwasher. And it was comforting. I knew I wasn't alone. There were people out there, people that cared about me. People that would keep me safe. But here in this cabin at the end of the world, there was no one out there, and there never would be anything ever again. Just me and Ben, and infinite entropy. Everything was empty.

I imagined Hector. It wasn't a hallucination, or computer image or whatever the hell he was, this was definitely just a daydream. I might have even been asleep. I imagined Hector standing above me, arms open, ready to pick me up and save me. In my dream, he had the wings of an angel.

Day 106:

I spent a lot of time in the garden, even on days when Ben didn't drive into town, or wherever it was he went. I was on my hands and knees with one of those little rakes that gardeners use. I didn't know what I was doing. Here I was, pretending to be a gardener. I'd never even kept a potted plant alive in my apartment for more than a week. Before Hector showed up and threw everything into doubt, I'd begun feeling a little pride in being able to figure things out. But had I? I was staring at a leaf, rubbing it gently between my fingers. Was it growing because I'd watered and pruned it properly? Was it only growing because it was just some video game thing programmed to grow and make me feel like I was winning? Make me content?

There was a drop of water beaded up on the leaf. I stared at the bead like it was a tiny snowglobe. Was there a universe inside? Could the tiny people inside that universe see me staring down at them from heaven? Another droplet appeared on the leaf. Then another, then another. The clouds above me opened up and a downpour started. I didn't move. I felt the rain hit my hair, my skin, my clothes. It felt real. It felt wet. Was I really dry and dusty in a lab somewhere, hidden under a sheet?

"Elyse?" Ben called out from the porch. "Elyse! Are you okay?" I watched the droplets run off the leaf, down my wrist, into the sleeve of my shirt. "Elyse?!?" Ben was there, next to me. He tapped me on my shoulder. I suppose, looking back, it must have been worrisome for him. Seeing me sitting like an idiot in the middle of a rainstorm, lost in my own thoughts. He shook me, and helped me to my feet. "Let's get you inside and dry you off by the fire," he said as he led me inside. "I'll make you some cocoa."

Day 110:

How long had it been? Two weeks maybe? Hector hadn't returned. Was he real? Had he ever been real? Something wasn't real. I think I once saw somebody in a cartoon say, "I'm the one thinking, so I'm the one who's real." Or something like that. Maybe that cartoon wasn't even real. My memory has never been all that great.

I stared at the cigarette in my hand, burned down to ash. I stared at the wool blanket on my lap, rough and firm. Out in the garden, fireflies were zooming back and forth. I think I could hear crickets in the distance. I moved my tongue around my mouth, feeling a sore from when I bit my cheek that morning chewing an apple. Was the pain real?

I glanced over at Ben, sitting silently across from me. He had a drink in his hand. He didn't speak. I didn't speak. Was he concerned? He seemed concerned. Concerned for what, though? That the one person he had in the world was a lunatic? That I was getting suspicious and figuring a way out of his trap? His face didn't betray his thoughts.

Maybe I should read a book. If this world wasn't real, then the book wouldn't be real, and so anything in it would be something my mind invented from my memory, that's what Hector said. And let's be honest, I'm not smart enough to make up a whole book. If I read a book, and it was *good*, then that'd mean it'd have to be real, right? Not something I made up.

There was music coming from the record player, another obscure jazz musician I didn't know. If evil genius Ben was pumping music in from outside, could he pump in the words to a novel too? Shit. Maybe. I wish Hector came back so I could ask him more questions about how all this worked.

Hector hadn't returned. If he was real, he would have come back by now, right? Would have tried again to warn me of the danger. Asked me if I'd learned anything that could help him. Or just to say hi and to make a joke and tell me something dumb to break the tension. He was always good at breaking the tension. But he wasn't here. Was that proof that Ben was right, that Hector was just a voice in my head? Maybe. Probably. No way to know. No way to know anything really. Were those crickets really out there, crawling around in the bushes? Or was I hearing static from a dead receiver?

Day 111:

Maybe I was feeling better that day. More energetic at least. Maybe the new pills Ben had found were higher quality and lifting my fog. I remember sitting at the kitchen table. Sunlight was streaming in from the window. I could see little specks of dust floating around in the sunbeam. Ben was clearing the dishes from breakfast.

"You didn't eat much of your pancakes," he said sweetly. I ate half a pancake. That was better than nothing, right? I didn't really respond, beyond maybe a nod or something. "Not eating isn't going to make you feel better, you know. Good nutrition is the key to good health, and I'm sure that your brain could do with some more vitamin B. I hear that vitamin B is...."

"I've never seen a dead body," I said blankly. Probably sounded creepy as hell, but I didn't really intend it that way. "I did a shoot once where there was a murder scene, and one of the PAs told me that real dead bodies look nothing like a guy just pretending to be dead. They're all discolored and bent into weird shapes."

"Um. Okay."

"Where are all the bodies, Ben? Tell me that?"

"The bodies?" Ben questioned.

"Yeah. Dead bodies. We're supposed to be living in the 'post-apocalypse' right? Shouldn't there be dead bodies all over the place? I've seen plenty of zombie movies. If everyone is dead, where are all the bodies?"

Ben squinched up half his face while he thought up an answer. "Well, I suppose they are all at home," he said. "Or maybe at the hospital somewhere? You know, it wasn't like a nuclear bomb or anything. No one just fell down and died instantly in the street. You and I felt sick and went home and went to bed. Probably everyone else did, too. They felt sick and closed up shop and went home. I bet that all the houses in town have bodies in their beds. Well... skeletons really by now. I'm not really sure how long it takes for someone to become a skeleton..."

I needed proof of the apocalypse. "I want to see one. I want to see a body." Maybe, as gross and scary as it sounded, seeing bodies lying all over the street would put my mind at ease.

"Elyse. I don't know if that's such a good idea. You aren't feeling all that well. I think that'd just get you upset."

"I want to see a body. Just to know that everyone is dead. Just to know. I want to see if they look different than what I think they look like."

Ben tried to laugh it off. "I think maybe you'd do better to just sit here and eat some vitamins. Maybe I could scramble you a couple of eggs?" I jumped up from the table and ran out through the front door. I could hear Ben behind me, "Elyse! Wait!" I started running faster. Full speed. The sound of my feet against the pavement of the street. I wasn't even wearing shoes. I could hear Ben's footsteps in the distance behind me. "Wait." He sounded farther and farther away. I was out of breathe.

I hadn't left the cabin since we "moved" out here months ago. There was a road that went for miles through the woods. I didn't remember much about the trip coming in. I didn't specifically know where the next house down the road would be. But it had to be somewhere. The cabin wasn't the only thing on this road. Or, if it was, eventually there would be another road, and another, that led to the city. My feet hurt.

I was panting heavily when I saw a mailbox up ahead. A driveway. I stopped, bent over, trying to catch my breath. So out of shape. I'd exercised all the time back before; when what I looked like mattered. I felt soft and pudgy. Ben's footsteps sounded closer. I looked back and saw him waving. I rolled my eyes and ran down the driveway to the house.

The home at the end of the driveway seemed intact, pristine. It wasn't caved in or on fire. I guess it had only been a few months, and so probably none of the windows had broken and the roof hadn't blown off. I wonder how long it takes for an abandoned house to start to look abandoned?

I needed to get inside. I needed to see a body. I needed to know that this wasn't a simulation of the world; that this *was* the world. I needed to know that even the gross and disgusting parts of it still existed. I needed to know that things didn't just end at an invisible wall, like they do in a video game. The real world goes on and on and on. Cities and towns and countries and continents, and it's all filled with houses and those houses are filled with things; couches, televisions, coffee mugs, nail clippers. If this was a video game and not real life, all those details would be missing, right?

I picked up a big potted plant that was near the front door. I lifted it up over my head and threw it at the big window. It bounced off and broke on the ground. I started banging my hands against the windowpane in frustration.

"Arrgh!"

By this point, Ben had caught up to me. "What are you doing, Elyse?" he said calmly.

"I'm trying to get into this damn house!" I hit the window again with my fists.

"If you try to get in that way, you'll cut yourself on the glass. And I don't know how to sew stitches. Maybe the door is open?" Ben jiggled the handle on the front door. It opened. He stepped aside and motioned for me to enter, like he was a hotel butler letting me into my room. I glared at him and walked inside.

The front door led to a living room. Everything in its place. There was some dust maybe, but that's it. An empty mug sat on the coffee table with a spoon still in it, its contents long dried away. No bodies, no one had died here. The air was stale maybe, but it wasn't putrid. I walked through into the dining room. There was a puzzle, half-finished, on the dining room table. It was a landscape, with a forest and a river, not too different from the view at our cabin. Still no bodies. Still nothing out of place.

I walked quickly past Ben, who by now was sitting nonchalantly on the living room couch, patiently waiting. Secretly judging me? I went upstairs. There was a hallway. Bathroom. Toothbrushes and makeup and towels. No bodies. All the bedroom doors were closed. I put my hand hesitantly on the doorknob. I remember closing my eyes and swallowing. Steeling myself for what might be on the other side. When I got super sick, I just went to bed. If I hadn't survived... Well, you know. Obviously, the bodies were probably going to be in the bedrooms.

I swung the door open violently and opened my eyes. It was a kid's room. A girl's. There were stuffed animals and some dolls, mostly tossed randomly on the floor. The bed had a sheet covered in stars and moons. It was neatly made. No one was in it, or under it, or in the closet, or hiding in the toy box. Maybe the sick kids were in bed with the sick parents? I guess that made sense.

I repeated the ritual of closing my eyes and swallowing and violently throwing the door open three more times. One room was another kid's bedroom. One was an office or something. The third was the parents' bedroom. Nothing. Bed made, things looking neat, more or less. No bodies. No sign of struggle, no sign anybody was sick, or dead, or anything. Was Hector right? He said that there were no bodies, and there were no bodies. But ok, if evil Benjamin had not bothered to put bodies in his simulation, then why bother to put anything inside the house at all? Why bother to add couches and toys and dust and mugs with spoons and half-done puzzles and all that other stuff? If he could add all that, then why not finish the illusion with a couple of skeletons?

But it was a dream, wasn't it? That was what Hector said. It wasn't a video game; it was a dream. And in dreams we make everything up ourselves. Everything that we *can* make up. And I know what a house looks like, and I know that it should have couches and toys and dust and mugs and puzzles and all that other stuff. So I guess I could be dreaming it? Right? But I don't know what a dead body looks like, except for in a zombie movie, and I'm pretty sure those don't look real. So my mind can't conjure up a realistic dead body. Hector said that was part of the limit to Ben's machine. It worked on dreams, or something.

I angrily swept all of the stuff off the dresser. Lamp, book, little bowl full of change; they all clattered to the floor. The lamp broke. It sounded real. The things bounced and rolled around on the floor like real things would bounce and roll around. "Elyse?" I heard Ben call from downstairs. I ripped all the covers off the bed and threw them to the floor. I threw the pillows against the wall. I tried to topple the dresser but it was too heavy. I grunted and cried in frustration. I turned over a nightstand, which made a loud bang when it fell.

"Elyse!" Ben shouted from the doorway. I had tears in my eyes. I pushed him out of the way and ran past him, back down the stairs. Where were the bodies? Was this real? Everything here made enough sense for me to think it was real, but then just enough was out of place and wrong that I doubted it. I ran through the living room and pushed all the lamps off the end tables. I picked up one corner of the dining room table and tipped the half-completed puzzle onto the floor.

Ben was following me, but from a distance. He was concerned enough to not want me to get hurt, but not assertive enough to grab me and slap me and tell me to get ahold of myself. "Where are they?" I shouted at him. "Where are the bodies!? What happened to the people living in this house!?" I threw open the cabinets under the kitchen sink. "Are they in here?!?" I shouted as I tossed the bottles of soap and furniture polish onto the floor. I threw open the cabinets above the counter. "Are they in here?!" I shouted as I pushed a whole stack of plates onto the floor. They clattered and shattered against the kitchen tiles. I closed my eyes, balled my fists, and breathed deeply, trying to regain my composure.

"Elyse." Ben said calmly from behind me. I turned around and wiped the tears from my face with my sleeve. Ben was standing there, looking at a handwritten note someone had left on the kitchen table. He read aloud, "Jasmine. We'll be on vacation until next Sunday night. The watering can is right by the sink, and I already showed you which plants need to get watered." He handed me the note. "Elyse, look." I took the paper from his hand. "They weren't here. They were on vacation somewhere. That's why there are no bodies in this house. The only person here that week was the housekeeper."

"Well... We'll go to the next house then," I grumbled. "And then the next one and the next one. One of these houses has to have someone..." All of a sudden, a small dog ran into the kitchen, barking and yapping. At once, I lost my train of thought.

"Hey there, little buddy," Ben said to the dog. Ben took a bag of treats that was sitting on the kitchen counter, opened it, and knelt down. He handed one to the dog, who greedily accepted.

"Oh my god," I said.

"Cute, huh? Poor thing must be so lonely without his family." He rubbed the dog's ears and handed him another treat.

"He looks just like Detective Stubbs!"

"Detective Stubbs?" asked Ben.

"It was a dog our family had when I was just a kid. I know, that was a stupid name. My brother named him. He's got stubby legs and our dad was a cop. My brother even made him a tiny badge to wear on his collar. It's been so long since I've seen a dog that looked like him."

"Well, you want this one? No reason to leave him here. It might be good for you to have some company." I came closer, gingerly avoiding all the shards of broken dishes everywhere. "Yeah. Yeah, I think I'd like that." I remember kneeling down and having Detective Stubbs come straight over to me. I rubbed him behind his ears. My hands unclenched.

Ben stood and came over to me, rolling up the bag of treats. "Let's give this up and go home now. You've had enough excitement. I've got pesto to make." He held out his hand to me. I looked up at him and smiled. "Things are going to be okay. I promise," he said. He wiped the tears from my cheeks with his sleeve.

Day 113:

Things got better after that. Ben was right. Honestly. I chalked the previous week up to another bad episode and moved on. That's the thing about my dumb brain, I'm fine for months at a time, and then the stress just gets to me and... I don't know. Everything swirls. My therapist explained that when people are telling me I'm acting crazy, I should write down all my thoughts on paper and explain to myself why I'm right and they are wrong. Then, wait a week and go back and read what I wrote. The idea was that the stuff in my head that seems so rational and sensible at the time might just be nonsense when viewed objectively later. I don't know what seeing a dead, rotting corpse would have proved to me. In retrospect, the idea sounds pretty dumb.

The land right around the house we lived in was heavily wooded, but you could walk down the road half a mile or so and get to a clearing. I started taking daily walks there with the new dog. I thought it was important to get out a little bit and not be cooped up in the same yard for weeks at a time. It also gave Ben a chance to have some alone time without me hovering around behind him. That's healthy in a relationship, right?

The clearing had a low, sloping hill that led down to the river. I'd sit at the top and just breathe. I'd taken some yoga classes at a trendy gym years ago. Breathe in, breathe out, nice and slow. Focus on yourself. "Be present," I was told. So I was doing my best to be present. I sat there on a rough woolen blanket with my legs crossed and just looked around me and felt the world as it existed at that very moment. I knew that a lot of the anxiety in the world comes (or I guess 'came'?) from people regretting about what happened in the past, or fretting about what was going to happen in the future. If you could forget about the past, forget about the future, and just keep your mind on what was in front of you, you'd be happy. That's the theory anyway.

Of course, easier said than done. Of course I regretted the past. All the words that I never got to say to the people close to me. Of course I fretted about the future. What would happen when Ben and I got too old? Or if one of us got cancer? And what was the point of anything anymore? Humanity was gone. Ben and I were the only two left. And soon enough we'd be gone too. And then there'd be no one left. No one to remember us, to remember all the impressive things we've done in life, all the fun times we'd had with friends and family. All of our experiences and hopes and dreams and plans would all be gone. Nothing, like they never even existed in the first place. Right now, in museums all around the world, there were beautiful pieces of art turning to mold and dust, never to be seen by human eyes again.

Push those thoughts out of your mind, Elyse. Just be here, just be now...

Stubbs had brought a ball with him. Thinking back, honestly I don't know where he found it. He just seemed to have it with him that day. Maybe Ben gave it to him. He dropped it right in front of me, but before I could pick it up, it just rolled down the hill all by itself. Stubbs chased after it, caught it, and ran back up the hill. He dropped it, let it roll down the hill, chased it, and brought it back to the top. Again and again, up and down.

I watched him zip back and forth. He was living in the moment. He wasn't worried about the time before or after. He wasn't worried that this was all a dream, or that there was somewhere outside of this place, some heaven somewhere. For the moment at least, he'd found his meaning, even if it was something dumb and simple like chasing a ball.

I wish I could be like that. Wish I could be happy just chasing a ball up and down a hill, over and over again. Some objectively pointless task that could take my mind off whatever might or might not be out there. Something to stop me from lamenting the fate of the world and how everything was lost. Then I realized, I could. It was within my power to define my own meaning, right? Everybody in the world had things that were important to them and things that weren't, right? Like, there are some people that really cared about collecting bottlecaps and it made their lives meaningful. But I didn't know anything about bottlecaps. I probably couldn't even name one famous bottlecap. But what I thought didn't matter to those collectors; they decided it was important and they found meaning in their collections, even if, at the end of the day, bottlecaps were objectively pointless things.

So, what should I decide was important? What should I decide made life worth living? Ben, of course... and Stubbs... and the seedlings in my garden. Those things had meaning. Maybe not in the grand scheme of the universe, but in the small part of the universe that was within my field of vision. I could live for them. Small things, sure, but maybe big enough to live for. Be here now, Elyse. Be here because those seedlings need you, Stubbs needs you, Ben needs you.

I breathed in deeply and felt the rough wool of the blanket against my legs. Stubbs took a break from his ball chasing to look up at me. I'd only known him a week or two and it was already clear that he cared about me, was dependent on me, he lived for me. I could live for him. I could live for Ben and the garden and our stupid little cabin, even if it didn't mean anything in the objective grand scheme of things. They were my bottlecaps. It was enough.

Day 124:

We were sitting on bank of the river. A little ways down from the cabin, someone had once built a small dock for their boat. The boat was long gone. Ben said it was a good place to fish. To be honest, the dock looked a little shaky to me, and I worried that if we both stood on it at once, it would collapse and we'd be washed away. Irrational, I know. But the riverbank near the dock was made of sand and pebbles and it was stable and soft to sit on. I remember I was wearing a large, floppy hat because it was sunny. I had intended to read a book that I had brought, but it lay unread as I leaned back, just enjoying the warm rays on my skin. I was throwing a stick to Stubbs the dog, who kept coming back to seek more attention from me, and I was getting occasionally distracted by Ben, who would now and then shout some sort of comment. Usually a pun about fish. Dumb dad-joke stuff. But he was trying to make me laugh. Trying to keep my spirits up. Trying to keep me sane. Trying to avoid another meltdown like the week before. The dog was helping. We'd also agreed to up the dosage of my meds, on account of the fact that they were maybe old and not as effective as fresh ones would be. I guess things were getting back to normal, as normal as our little family could be here at the end of the world. Or at least, it felt that way.

I got up to stretch my legs. I had some rocks in my hand, and I threw them into the water one by one as I walked down the riverbank. I could hear Ben's voice fading in the distance, although he wasn't really all that far away. He was singing a stupid song that he was making up as he went along... about fish.

I remember hearing a rustling sound coming from the trees. But, like I told you before, it wasn't... right. It was more like some radio station was playing rustling noises, but the receiver wasn't quite tuned into the exact frequency. I swallowed and tried to ignore it. I threw another rock into the water. More rustling. I spun around suddenly and launched a rock into the trees. It disappeared into the dense leaves, and there was a 'clunk' sound as it bounced off an unseen trunk. The rustling stopped. I took a few more steps and there was another rustle. Closer this time. I spun around to throw another rock, and Hector was standing not five feet away from me.

"Elyse, there you are! I'm sorry it's taken so long to find you again." I threw the rock at his head, but missed on purpose. "Did you learn anything about where he's keeping you?" I turned back around and tried to stomp off. "I'm trying to save you, but I need you to help me," I heard him shout from behind me.

"Get out of my head!" I threw another rock into the water and tried to ignore him.

"I'm not in your head. I'm right here. Well, I'm in some room at the crime lab with this goofy contraption attached to my face, but I'm as real as anything else in this world. More real in fact, because I'm not computer generated."

"No, you are just my dumb brain making me see things again." I started mumbling to myself, "Got to stay strong, Elyse, got to stay strong. Don't listen to things that aren't real..."

"Dammit, I'm not a hallucination!" Hector said, voice full of conviction. Or what I interpreted to be conviction anyway.

I closed my eyes, but he didn't go away. "You are... you're not real."

"Why? Because Benjamin says I'm not?"

I opened my eyes and Hector was standing directly in front of me. "No. Yes. But no. I've had hallucinations before. I take all these drugs to stop them, but the drugs don't work anymore. So you are just a hallucination." Sure, I could see him and hear him and I wanted him to be real, I mean, how could I not? But c'mon, the story was a bit crazy, don't you think? And, my counsellors always said that if something sounds unbelievable, it probably isn't real, even if you can see it.

"Elyse, I'm your brother. I know all about your medical history. Don't you remember that time I came home from school, and you were hiding under your desk screaming and banging your head against the wall, and we took you to the hospital? Or the time I found you walking barefoot down the street, dazed, in the middle of winter? Or that time we came to visit you in that in-patient treatment center in Arizona? I was there for all of your little episodes."

"That's just what a hallucination would say." How can anyone trust anything? That's the insidious thing about being delusional, the delusions will do their best to convince you they aren't delusions.

"I know you, you're my sister. You know I know you."

I had to believe in this world. I had to trust that things which didn't make sense weren't real, even if they told me what I wanted to hear. "You are just like a dream, Hector. Just because you tell me things I already know, that doesn't mean you aren't just in my head."

81

Hector cocked his head to the side, as if he was listening to someone talking to him. He nodded. "Okay. Okay." He said to the unseen person. He turned toward me. "I can prove it. The dog. The dog proves that I'm not a hallucination."

"The dog?"

"Yeah, the dog. It looks just like Detective Stubbs doesn't it? I mean it *really* looks like my old dog Detective Stubbs. Right down to that mis-colored white patch of fur behind his left ear." He knelt down and looked like he was about to pet the dog, but he stopped just short. "Good to see you again, boy," Hector said with a wistful smile on his face. He stood back up. "This isn't some random dog— it *is* Detective Stubbs. Or at least, it's your best recollection of him. Remember what I told you about how the machine works? It doesn't generate pixels, it sends your brain concepts and your brain fills in the details. All Benjamin did was feed in the *concept* of a dog, and your brain is interpreting that data to look like a dog you already know."

"But Benjamin saw it, too. And you see it."

"It's your world, Elyse. Benjamin and I and anyone else who logs in can interact with it, but it's all stuff created from your mind."

"If it's my world, why can't I make you just go away?"

"I told you, I'm not computer-generated," he said glibly.

I screamed in frustration and started to stomp away. I could hear Hector following me. "Benjamin put the dog in as a distraction because you were starting to challenge the simulation. That could have crashed the system and caused you to wake up. He doesn't want you to wake up. He wants things to be perfect for you here, that's why there are no dead bodies. Dead bodies are messy and scary and he doesn't want you to feel those emotions. He just wants you to be content."

I continued stomping away purposefully. "I am content. This life, it's so easy. There's no rejection from casting directors, or worrying about money, or dealing with Mom's criticism, or creepy stalkers, or any of that."

He kept following. "Too easy, though. Suspiciously easy. All your problems gone away and nothing to do day after day but tend your garden and spend time with a sweet, non-threatening boyfriend. Do you think the end of the world would really be like this?"

"Sure, why not?" I replied. "There're whole supermarkets full of food and gas stations full of fuel for the generators. It's not like zombies are roaming the streets, or aliens in the sky. Why can't it be easy? Why can't my life be easy for once? And I'm tired of you, I'm tired of everyone not having faith in me, not believing I can do it. I *can* do it. Every day I'm proving to my dumb brain that I'm strong enough to succeed and my dumb brain keeps sending you to make me feel bad." I spun around and threw my last rock at his head. "Screw you!" It missed.

"You've got to wake up, Elyse. I know that you think it's great here in your pristine little stress-free world with your childhood dog and ripe red tomatoes growing on the vine and a perfect, supportive, non-threatening partner to share it all with, but you can't stay here forever. This place is going to destabilize." Hector sounded so sincere. Sounded so real. Real things always sound real. But hallucinations and delusions also sound

83

real. Sometimes even realer than real. Realer than how real things sound, I mean. "I know you are worried about your meds. Real-world Benjamin doesn't have any real drugs for your real body. You're totally off your meds right now; you have been ever since you woke up here, despite you taking whatever simulated pills he's been handing you. And you and I both know, the longer you are off those things, the more unstable you become, and this whole world is built on your brain, your dumb, broken brain. Things are going to start getting weird here soon. It's going to all collapse around you."

I started to run back towards the dock. Stubbs was chasing after me, just like a real dog would. Would a ghost dog run like that? A computer dog? A hallucination dog? Hector didn't try to follow, but I could hear him shouting at me, getting further and further away. "Elyse! You have to listen to me. The world hasn't ended. You just need to open your eyes. Have faith that we're out here waiting for you. Just open your eyes!"

I realized I was running with my eyes tightly shut. Trying to block Hector out, trying to block everything out. Trying to block the world out. I opened them so I wouldn't trip. Ben was right in front of me, he'd come looking for me. He was holding a large dead fish, still dripping wet.

"Check it out! Fresh fish for dinner, baby!" he said with an innocent smile. I turned around, but Hector was nowhere in sight. His voice had faded to nothing. The only sound was the rustling of the wind through the leaves. "Hey, you okay?" Ben said.

"I'm fine," I replied. "Let's go back inside, it's getting dark."

Day 125:

There was still leftover fish that next morning. Ben always woke before me. He was usually in the kitchen cooking breakfast by the time I came down the stairs in my snuggly flannel bathrobe. He always seemed excited to be making breakfast. It made me feel guilty. Why was he the one who always cooked, and cleaned, and did the housework? At first, when we moved into this cabin together, I did a lot. I decorated things and moved the furniture around, I read through cookbooks and experimented with different recipes. I washed the dishes. I guess in those first weeks, I wanted to be useful; I was still scared about the end of the world, that if we didn't fight fight fight to survive, we'd die. Then, after it became clear that we weren't going to die, I kept doing things out of a desire to please Ben. I wanted to make him happy. Honestly. Be the perfect housewife. It made me feel good to do things for someone whom I cared about. It still makes me feel good to do things for someone I care about. I guess. After seeing Hector for the first time though, I found I started to lose interest in fighting, in cleaning, in cooking, in moving. The strength of the feeling came and went, but it was always there. And as days went by, I slowed, then stopped, doing things. I just didn't have the energy. And every time I slowed down, Ben sped up. He took over more of the cooking, more of the cleaning. He tried to weed the vegetable garden. He seemed to have more and more energy. I guess he was just doing his best to be supportive; to pick up the slack for what I can only assume he thought was just a temporary dip in my energy level.

At first, seeing him do all the work made me feel bad about my sluggishness, and I pushed myself to try harder. And I did try harder. But it got harder and harder to try harder. So, I stopped pushing myself. And I got down on myself. I was a lump and I felt guilty that Ben was taking up all the slack, and working twice as hard because I wasn't pulling my weight. Worst of all, I started to resent him for helping me because his brightness only made my shadow seem darker. But we talked about it and I confessed that I was a failure and a wreck and it wasn't fair to him and blah blah blah. And he said something really interesting. He told me that he *liked* doing things for me. That it wasn't a chore for him to cook or clean, he *wanted* to be useful and to be helpful and to do stuff. It made him feel good. And he told me to stop worrying about him and just focus on myself. It took me a few days to get used to it, but I just decided to let it go. To let him do what he wanted to do. I wasn't going to keep letting myself feel guilty about it.

But anyway, I'm getting off track. I was talking about that specific morning. Ben had made some kind of omelet or something from the leftover fish. I barely ate any of it. I was just staring into space, sipping some tea. I remember those mornings because the sun really streamed in from the windows, and the steam from the tea was bright and mesmerizing as it drifted through the sunbeams. Ben was clearing off the dishes. As he grabbed my plate, he said, "So, I was thinking. Maybe we should take up a hobby."

"A hobby?" I said, only half-listening. I didn't even look at him. I was focused on the wisps of tea steam.

"Yeah. Like, if you had asked me before all of this happened what my life after the apocalypse would be like, I'd probably have said that it would be really hard and intense, but you know, it hasn't been. Maybe it's the lack of zombies."

"Zombies?"

"Zombies, mutants, aliens, whatever." Ben said. "The only apocalypses you ever see in the movies is when there's a zombie attack, or some giant solar flare nuclear winter. And the survivors have to fight in some desolate wasteland to stay alive. But it's not really like that. Ironic. I mean, there's more than enough food for us to eat, and plenty of spare parts to keep this shelter going. And the only scary thing so far is when that bear wandered through the garden last month, remember that? The bear?"

"I remember the bear."

"And we just scared him off by banging some pans. So anyway, yeah, a hobby. Like maybe we could do something to make things a little less dreary around here. I was thinking of maybe getting a guitar? I've never been all that musical, but I've got nothing but time these days. Can't be harder than the ukulele, right? I can learn the guitar and you could, I don't know, learn to play the piano or the bassoon or whatever, and we could write songs for each other. That could be fun. It'll help take your mind off whatever's been bothering you."

"I don't think playing the bassoon will help." I wasn't sure what would help. What's the point of writing songs that no one besides the two of us would ever hear?

Ben finished putting the dishes in the sink. He came back and pulled the chair I was sitting in away from the table. He got down on his knees in front of me and took both of my hands in his. "I know. I get it. I'm not dumb. I know you are lonely. You're a famous actress and probably used to going to the fanciest parties and palling around with models and cool people on red carpets. And now all you've got is one goofy nerd to spend time with. How can you not be lonely?"

I shook his hands out of mine and stood up. "It's not... loneliness. I don't know, I just feel trapped. Like I'm suffocating. Like this isn't how my life is supposed to be. It's all this time. All this time to think. Every day, nothing to do, no appointments to go to. Just time. Time to realize that everything here is meaningless. If we are the only ones left, what's the point of anything?"

I walked out the front door in my bare feet. I needed some air. I stood on the porch outside of the cabin, with my arms crossed, staring up into the sky. I remember looking to see if any birds were flying past, but there were no birds, only some clouds drifting by. One passed in front of the sun and all the beams of light disappeared. It suddenly seemed a bit colder. Ben gave me a few minutes of space and then followed me out on the porch, holding a cup of coffee. He put his hand on my shoulder. I remember looking down at his hand, and he removed it awkwardly.

"I wish things were different, too, you know." He said. "But it's not like I planned this."

"Why did we get so lucky? Why us? Don't you feel guilty?" I think it was summertime that day, but it felt cold. The sun gave no warmth.

"I don't know if I'd use the word 'guilty.' 'Fortunate' maybe? I don't know why it was us. But I can't feel guilty about being alive. I didn't unleash the plague. I wasn't in charge of the quarantine. I was just a lowly drone working in a random office."

"I guess I'm just having a hard time. This world. Everything is different. Everyone is dead. Do you ever stop to think about that? Really think about that? Everyone is dead. All those kids you knew in grade school, that cashier at the supermarket that always asked about your day. They are all dead."

Ben looked up at the sky with me. "I know. I think about it, too. At night, when you think I'm sleeping and you get up out of bed and stare out the window, I'm awake, too. Thinking about how it's all empty out there. Just wilderness now. You know how worried I am that I'm not going to be able to protect you, protect us?"

I turned to him, "How do you do it? How do you make it through the night? The silence. Knowing there's nothing out there. Nothing anywhere out there?"

"How do I do it?" he said in disbelief. He glanced downward, and gave a hearty laugh. "It's you, Elyse. You are how I do it. I'd be a complete wreck if it weren't for you. I need you. You are my rock. You are the thing that gives my life meaning. That's why I'm so scared about losing you. I wouldn't be able to make it without you. No way."

"Before we met, I was up on that bridge..."

"Don't think I haven't thought about that, too. Don't think I wouldn't be up on that bridge in a minute if you ever left. I couldn't do it alone." He looked scared. He looked vulnerable. He looked like *he* needed *me*, not the other way around. I wasn't the burden, I was the inspiration. He was living for me. "He who has a *why* to live for can bear almost any *how*," he whispered. It didn't matter to him that the universe was absurd, all that mattered to him was me. That was enough.

"But I'm not going to be here forever." I said to him.

"I know," he replied. "But so? We have right now. That's enough." I fell into his arms and pressed my cheek against his chest. "And you know what the weirdest part of this apocalypse is?" he said, draping his arms around my shoulders, "I'm way happier these days than I've ever been before. And that's not just because I don't have to deal with all those assholes in the office and wait in line at the bank anymore. It's because I'm in love. Really in love. Truly. I can't explain it. Out of all the people to be stuck with at the end of the world, I ended up with the most beautiful, the most perfect one."

I'm pretty sure I had tears in my eyes. "I think the luckiest part of all this was meeting you. You treat me with so much respect, so much caring. I've never had that before. I had a lot of boyfriends. I mean a *lot* of boyfriends. But they were all self-absorbed jerks. Maybe that's just because they were mostly actors. It's a very narcissistic profession."

"As one of those 'nice guys' you always hear about, I always wondered why beautiful girls like you always dated jerks instead of giving computer geeks like us a chance."

I felt the hair stand up on the back of my head. I pushed him away from me. "Computer geeks?"

"I meant, geeks in general. Like nerds, dorks. I don't know why I said computer geeks. There's lots of other kinds of geeks I suppose." He said it so naturally.

Was that the slip Hector warned me to look for? Was it just my imagination? I looked him in the eyes to see if there were any signs he was lying. But then I admitted to myself that I had no idea what signs I should be looking for. He wasn't squinting or anything. He wasn't sweating.

"Law geeks?" Maybe it wasn't a slip up.

"Yeah. Lawyers can be geeks, too. Up late at night, on the internet, arguing about the constitution and stuff."

"You did that?" Was I right to be suspicious of that slip, or was it all in my imagination? Maybe it was just my imagination.

"Would you hate me if I did?"

"I'd find it endearing."

He paused a second, to make it look like he was lying. "Then yes. I did that all the time. I admit it." He really did nerd-out like that though. You could tell. I pushed him playfully.

"No, you didn't," I said, chuckling.

"Okay, you're right. It's worse. I was up late, on the internet, arguing about video games and sci-fi movies."

"That's more like it."

Ben turned back towards the yard, and resumed looking up at the sky. "Ugh. I miss geeking out to a good sci-fi movie. I still listen to movie soundtracks sometimes when I'm driving to Lake Clark." Wait.

"Lake Clark? Is that where you are going every day? Why are you driving all the way to Lake Clark? That's like an hour away at least?"

"I meant... that one time I drove down to Lake Clark." This time it definitely sounded like a slip up. Like he was hiding something.

91

"That doesn't make any sense," I said flatly.

"There are... a lot of... farms there." I remember that he stammered. He definitely stammered. "I mean, there *were* a lot of farms there. I figured, I don't know, you know, maybe if there were people around they'd cluster in some farmland area?" He paused, I could see he was trying to choose his words carefully as to not trigger me. "There wasn't anybody there, though. It was overgrown. I almost ran over a cow that got loose somehow." I remember thinking that he was definitely slipping up.

I grew more alarmed. "What the hell is in Lake Clark?!?"

Ben's response seemed angry. "I told you," he said. "Nothing is in Lake Clark. I just went there once. Jesus. I've been all over the place looking for stuff for you. Food, clothing, other people. I go all over." He turned from me and waved his hands in the air. But I pressed the issue.

"But you didn't say that. You didn't say 'all over.' You said Lake Clark. Specifically Lake Clark." Maybe I shouldn't have pressed the issue. Why was I trying to make him angry?

I watched his back rise and fall for several deep breaths. Then he turned back around, with a smile on his face. "Look, I don't know why I said Lake Clark. I didn't mean anything by it." He didn't appear angry at all. Maybe I just read more into it than was really there.

"It's just a weird thing to say."

"I..."

"You see why I'd be suspicious."

"Suspicious of *what*, Elyse?"

"I don't know." Maybe it sounds dumb, but I think I actually felt a little guilty for upsetting him.

"There's nothing for me to hide from you." He put his hands on my shoulders and smiled.

I guess I didn't know if he was lying or not lying. If this was the clue to everything or not a clue to anything. But whatever it was, there was nothing to gain by continuing to nag him about it. I decided to play it off as a joke and think about it later. "I guess not," I said, "It's not like you could have another girl down there...."

"I mean... nothing except my *other family*...!" Ben said, joking right back at me.

"Your other family?" I said, over-exaggerating my 'shocked' face. "I knew it! Is she prettier than me?"

"Well...." Ben shrugged adorably. I playfully started hitting him. He ran back inside the house. I chased him around, playing like I was upset.

"How dare you cheat on me. I bet she's a hussy!" We chased each other around the furniture for a bit, laughing and screaming in mock anger, until we got tired. We both collapsed on the couch when we were spent.

After a minute of catching our breath, Ben jumped back up. "Okay, well. I think I'm going to finish washing up the dishes. Let's pop open a glass of champagne afterwards and have a toast. For no particular reason."

"Sounds great!" I said, still chuckling. Ben walked into the kitchen and left me to my own devices. I tried to regulate my emotions for a bit, but I had a hard time. I knew the pills weren't working anymore. I remember feeling my laughter becoming slower and slower with each giggle and starting to sound crazier and crazier. I felt the muscles in my face change into a look of worry. I felt my body slide lower and lower into the

couch, then onto the floor. Then into a ball. I was
crying hysterically. Ben didn't see.

Day 126:

The next day was cold and grey. I don't think that Ben was around that morning, but to be honest, I don't know where else he would have been, so I'm sure he was nearby somewhere. I was sitting on the picnic table outside of the cabin. I was staring off into the distance. Staring at the river. Were there fish in the river? Hidden under the surface? If you could move all the water out of the way, how many fish would appear? Five? A hundred? A thousand?

I knew Hector was standing behind me. I could feel him, the way you feel the static electricity when you get near a fuzzy sweater or a balloon someone's been rubbing. I took a drag on my cigarette and stamped it out on the table. Every day, they tasted staler and staler.

"This isn't real, is it?" I said to him, or maybe to no one in particular. "None of this is real."

I heard his voice behind me. "That's what I've been saying, Elyse."

"Did I just want it to be real? Did I just want to escape?"

"None of this is what you wanted. This is what he wanted. You can't...."

"No. I wouldn't be here if I didn't want this. I accepted it, didn't I? I just accepted it." Did I even try to check things out? Go to my parents' home to see if they were okay? Knock on a neighbor's door? No... I don't remember ever doing that. I got up and wandered into the garden. Hector must have followed.

"It's not like you really had an option. This world is really convincing. I can see it too, you know. It all looks real. Those chickens, that cabin, those tomatoes."

I wandered among my plants. A tomato was growing. Almost ripe. I picked it, and felt its firm skin between my fingers. I could almost smell its tartness. "I thought I had a green thumb. I was pretty proud of myself. Look at these. They are big and juicy and way better than what I used to buy."

"You can start a garden in the real world, once we get you out. I'll help. It'll be great."

"Maybe," I said, tossing the fresh tomato onto the soil.

"What finally gave it away?"

"Inconsistencies. Things he said, I guess. It didn't add up. He let it slip that he's a computer geek. But he said before that he was a lawyer. I don't know. Maybe I misread it. He joked about it. Maybe it was just poor wording. But then he started talking about Lake Clark."

"Lake Clark?" Hector said with interest. "What about Lake Clark?"

"Just that he goes there sometimes. But there's no real reason to go there, is there? It's just a little town and it's far away. I tried to call him out on it, but he just said he misspoke. But people don't really misspeak like that. I don't think I do anyway. I wouldn't have said Lake Clark unless it meant something to me. I figured it must mean something to him."

"That's a good lead. It makes sense that he wouldn't try to hide you too close to the city. He's smart enough to cover his tracks."

"What are you going to do now?" I imagined what this place would look like when the computer was shut down. I pictured the clouds falling out of the sky, and the trees sinking into the ground. All of the unripe vegetables in the garden blinking out of existence, one by one. Stars fall like pixels. The sky turns black. The ground disappears. Nothing is left. Except for me, and my dog. Stubbs looks up at me, not understanding what is happening, and then he too melts away. Just me now. Then darkness. Then what? I ascend into a higher dimension? Wake up somewhere new? Heaven? Strapped to a machine in a dusty closet? Back to my old life, filled with backstabbing friends and expensive coffee and sweaty gyms and traffic jams and...

"Lake Clark is a small place." Hector said. "We'll find you."

"Will you hurt him?" I wondered out loud.

"Jesus, Elsie! He kidnapped you!"

"I just mean, don't hurt him, okay? He's never done anything to hurt me." Hector didn't respond. I remember back when I was a kid, and I used to say crazy things, and little Hector used to call me out on it. Try to get me to admit I was wrong. Try to get me to say I was crazy, that there was no monster under the bed trying to eat me. That I wasn't being chased down the street by men in black. That there was no voice coming over the unplugged radio. Eventually, he got a stern talking to by Mom and Dad. I know they told him to shut up. "Let Elyse be crazy. You just make it worse when you challenge her." Hector rarely challenged me after that. He would just nod and wait until the crazy passed, and leave it to some doctor to talk to me about it later. Although you could always tell when he was biting his tongue.

But I also remember that my feelings for Ben *were* genuine. I mean, I don't know, did I really think at the time that he was a kidnapper? Maybe, probably... I guess? But he never hit me, or hurt me, or said cruel things to me, or made me feel bad or sad or small or dumb. Even when I did dumb things. I couldn't say that about most of the other guys I dated. Didn't that earn him a little kindness from me?

You usually could hear the engine from a mile away. His was the only car on the road. But this time, I guess I didn't hear it. Not until it suddenly appeared coming down the driveway. I was kind of frozen in place. The car stopped, and Ben jumped out, full of energy.

"Elyse!" He said as if nothing at all was wrong. "I think I may have found some evidence of someone. I was out by the mall. Not the mall near us, that other mall, the small one that no one ever goes to. What the hell was it called? Anyway, there was this car crashed into a pole. The door was open. I don't remember seeing that the last time I was out there, so maybe it's new? But why would anyone be crashing cars into poles? Maybe for fun? I don't know. Maybe the parking brake finally failed and it just rolled. But if so, then why was the door open? But who knows? I left a note. I'll go back there over the next few weeks and see if I can't find any more evidence. I don't want to get your hopes up but... wait... what's wrong?" He looked directly into my eyes, as if the thing that was wrong was within me somewhere, and not standing right over my shoulder.

I turned and looked at Hector. He was still here. I turned back to Ben. I probably said something like, "Uh."

Hector announced loudly, "Of course he can see me. He can hear me. He is pretending not to."

"...why..." I was confused.

Ben looked confused. too. "Why what?" he said.

Hector continued. "He's pretending not to see or hear me because he wants to convince you I'm just a delusion."

I got it together. "Stop lying to me, Ben," I scolded him. "I know this isn't real. Just let me go. I promise, if you just let me go, I won't press charges. This is wrong."

There was a look of shock on his face. "What are you talking about?" He said, like he had no idea what I was talking about. But this world wasn't real. It couldn't have been real. I caught him in the lie about Lake Clark.

"What you are doing... it's just weird." I told him, "Why would you do this? You're a nice guy, really. You could have just found someone...."

"Oh god. You think you're dreaming again," he replied. "Elyse, focus... stay with me..."

I remember hearing Hector speaking from behind me. "Don't let him near you. Look at that device in his hand." It all happened so fast. Was Ben holding something?

I started to lose it. Dumb brain. Panic attack. "It *is* a dream." I heard myself droning on and on, but it sounded like the voice was coming from somewhere else, like I wasn't inside my own body. "This world is stupid. You are stupid. I can't live here anymore, I can't breathe, I can't be here. I'm not supposed to be here. I'm not supposed to be the only one still alive. There's a whole wide world out there where things are actually real, where people are still here, where stuff matters. You need to let me go."

Ben moved towards me. He reached out to try to stabilize me. I was dizzy. "Elyse, you're having an episode. It's okay. We'll get through this. You just need..."

Everyone started shouting over each other. A jumble of words. I could hear Hector shout, "It's a reset switch!"

I could hear my own voice scream, "Stay away from me! Hector! Keep him..."

I could hear Ben, too. "You just need to take your pills. I've got some right here, I keep some just in case..."

Hector sounded resigned. "I can't do anything. Nothing that happens here matters." I could see Ben moving towards me. He had something in his hand. Maybe it was a pill bottle. I guess, thinking back on that day, it could have been a pill bottle. But maybe it was something else. Or maybe it was nothing. I couldn't see clearly.

As Ben got closer, I shouted for Hector. But he was faded. I could see through him. A ghost? A mirage? A delusion? An angel? He looked like he was getting further and further away even though he was right there next time me.

"Elyse! There is no Hector. Hector's dead." Ben said. His voice was stern. Trying to bring me back to reality. No, trying to take control. No, trying to save me. No, trying to confuse me. No.

"Hector is right here," I said. I tried to point in Hector's direction, but it was like I couldn't look at him directly. He was only in focus when he was in the corner of my eye.

"There's no one there, it's just the two of us. We're all that's left!"

I pleaded with Ben. "I know you can see him. He says you can see him. We know all about what you've done. The police are looking for me. They are coming to save me..."

"There's no one there!" He picked up a rock and threw it in the direction I was pointing. It missed. Hector didn't flinch.

I watched as Hector completely faded out of reality. The last words I could hear him say, like they were shouted from down a long tunnel, were "Nothing that happens here matters. Remember that. It's all a dream. I know where to look now. I'll see you soon when you wake up in the real world. I promise."

I spun back around, and Ben was right next to me. He grabbed my arm roughly. Everything went black.

Day 128:

I awoke with a start, as if someone had just shaken me. My eyes snapped open, tearing the half-encrusted lids apart. It was daylight out. I was on my side, turned away from the window, but even the reflection of the sun against the wall was so bright that it made me squint. Maybe I'd just been asleep for too long.

I attempted to shift position, still entangled in the covers. "Good morning," I heard someone say sweetly. I rolled over to see who it was. Benjamin. He was sitting in a comfy chair. Our bedroom. He was reading a book. A big one, like the kind you read in college. "Good morning," he said again.

I jumped back and curled up at the head of the bed. Like a cat does when it sees a snake. Primal fear. Ben calmly closed the book, slid off his chair and knelt down at the foot of the bed. "Shhh... shhh...," he said gently. "It's okay Elyse. You're safe."

"Ben. What the hell...?"

"I made tea. It's a little cold now, but I can warm it up if you'd like. Chamomile. One sugar." He gestured to the nightstand. There was a mug and a small bowl of fresh berries.

"How did I get here?" The last I remember, I was... I was.... Actually, at the time I didn't really remember what happened. I guess now, looking back, I can piece things together, but that morning, I was confused and groggy.

"You had a psychotic break, I think." Ben handed me the textbook. "Look it up yourself." The title was 'Clinical Psychiatry' or something like that. "I think the meds have been a bit off. I was trying to compensate for the fact that they are getting old and maybe I prescribed too much. Or... not enough. I'm sorry, I'm not an expert on this stuff. We'll get it worked out."

"Leave me alone. Get out! Hector! Hector!" I tried to recoil further away, but there wasn't any place to go.

Ben, to his credit, didn't try to approach me, or tell me to get a hold of myself, or slap me the way men slap hysterical women in the movies. He shifted back from me, gave me space. Calmly, he said, "Hector's not here. He's never been here. It's a hallucination, but I get that he totally *feels* real. I'm telling you that I believe you saw him, and you heard him tell you things. Things that in a crazy way made a lot of sense. But you've got to understand that it's just the chemicals in your head misfiring. It's not real." He pointed over to a place on the floor where there was now a big pile of other textbooks. "Trust me. You've been out for almost 24 hours. I drove over to the college bookstore and got every psych book I could find. I haven't slept. Everything that you've been ranting about is like a textbook sign of a psychotic break. Read it for yourself if you don't believe me."

I didn't know how to respond. Everything had been getting clearer for weeks, and then all of a sudden it got fuzzy again. I didn't feel good. And it wasn't the 'stomach bug' or 'post-workout' not feeling good; it was the 'my dumb brain acting up and making me see things again' kind of not feeling good. I just stared at the wall silently for like, I don't know, a whole minute, trying to get my thoughts together, but nothing came to me. I looked over to Ben and his gaze locked to mine.

103

"There's obviously nothing I can do or say to prove anything to you," he said. "You're going to have to come to your decisions on your own. I can't force you to do anything, and if I tried, it'd only make things worse. So, you are just going to have to figure it out yourself. In the meantime, have some tea."

"How can you be so calm?" I asked.

"What other choice do I have?" he half-chuckled. "I'm not calm, I'm freaking out on the inside, but I don't really have any other option, do I? There's no one I can ask for help with this, and I can't put you away in an asylum or send you back to your Mom's house or anything. We are stuck together. And me getting upset or yelling or trying to defend myself from your hallucinations won't make anything better. It'll make it worse. So, I'm pretending everything is great and normal because that's all I can think to do." He stopped talking and gave me time to process what he had just said. He looked around the room. Was he thinking to himself about how unlucky he must have been; that the last woman on earth was some kind of crazed maniac? I don't know what he was actually thinking. It is impossible to ever know what anyone is really thinking. After a time though, he started talking again. "Here's the thing, Elyse. If your brother is really out there in some 'real world,' he would've rescued you by now. And he hasn't. Where is he?"

"I... I don't know."

"And how would he even know where to look? If you just disappeared, why would he possibly think that you'd been kidnapped by some kind of mad scientist? He'd be looking for you in drainage ditches or stuffed into a trash can in a back alley. He wouldn't be part of a team of scientists hacking into some signal on the internet, right? I mean, come on, try to imagine what your story sounds like; it's crazy right? You have to be able to see that you sound crazy."

"I don't know!" I shouted at him. There were tears in my eyes again.

"Okay, okay. I'm sorry. Look at it this way, either this is the real world or it's not, right? If this is the real world you've got to start accepting it. Or if it's like he said, and 'nothing really matters' in here, then you might as well have some tea while you wait." He reached over, picked up the teacup of the bedside table, and offered it to me. "I know how lonely you are being stuck here with just me to talk to," he said gently.

"It's not that. It's just... everything seems so improbable, you know? How could this be real? Out of all the places I thought I'd be, this was never somewhere I'd considered."

"Do you even want your old life back?"

"Sometimes. Sometimes I want it more than anything. Other times, I don't want it at all." I put the teacup down. The tea was cold.

"You don't even know what you want and you are driving yourself crazy thinking about all the things you don't have," said Ben. "I miss everyone, too, but things are pretty good here in our little cabin, aren't they? You've said that multiple times."

"They are."

"And I know nothing really matters anymore. There aren't awards to win or people to impress. You can't become famous or successful or rich. But who cares? We make our own meaning. Life may be small here in this little Eden we've built at the end of the world, but I'm happy here with you. And I think you are happy here with me. I'm focused on *us*, here, living

105

day by day. That's what gives me energy to get up every morning."

"It's hard to let go of the things I've always thought were important. After all those years struggling to make a name for myself, to get ahead, to be the person I thought everyone wanted me to be." I said.

"You get to decide what's important to you, Elyse. That's what's cool about being a sentient being. If you just make a conscious decision that your garden is important, that this cabin is important, that I'm important, well, that's enough to give yourself the energy to get out of bed every morning. You just have to commit to your decisions. The only things meaningful in life are the things that we decide to give meaning to, either intentionally or unintentionally. You have a strong mind, so use your willpower to make your decisions intentionally. You'll be happier in the end." He smiled.

I thought back to my day sitting in the clearing, watching my dog run back and forth with that ball. The dog didn't care what anybody else thought, or about what was important in the grand scheme of the universe. I agreed with Ben's perspective, I suppose. He seemed happy. He was way less stressed and worried about the future and the past than I was. Let it go. I looked about the room. It was a warm, comfortable space, filled with things I cared about. What more did I need to be happy? I should be happy here. I was going to be happy here. I sipped the lukewarm tea Ben had made for me.

Ben stood up. "I'm going to go downstairs and clean up a bit. Maybe make you some eggs if you are up for it. Then I'm going to take a nap. Sit, rest, drink some tea. Read a few of those psych books. I've bookmarked some of the pages. Up on the nightstand is

106

a new kind of pill you might want to try. There's a bottle of water. Get yourself centered. Then, when you are ready, come downstairs. I've got a surprise for you."

"A surprise?"

"Well, a trip, I guess. I want to take you around and show you some things."

Still Day 128:

Later that day, I was washed and dressed and standing on a street corner in a city. I hadn't been to a city since soon after I met Ben. We were standing on a street corner looking up at a building.

"Welcome to downtown Lake Clark," Ben said.

"Why are we here?"

Ben pointed at a store across the street from the building we had come here to look at. "Well, first, I guess I wanted to show you that pharmacy over there on the corner. That's where I've been getting your new meds."

"You come all the way out here?" I said in disbelief.

"Well, they've got the best prices!" Ben gave a goofy smile. I just stared at him expressionless. He did one of those 'ba-da-bing' things and said, "That was a joke." I continued staring at him blankly. I was feeling better than I'd been that morning, but I wasn't ready for jokes just yet. Sometimes Ben's goofiness was cute and adorable, other times it was just annoying. "Okay, okay," he said, "I wanted to take you to this specific building here."

"What's in that building?"

"It's just easier if I showed you." I crossed my arms and sighed. "Nothing dangerous or scary, I swear." I didn't move. Ben had said that morning that he wanted to show me 'some things,' but he refused to explain what he meant. That was annoying. "You promised you were going to try," he said.

"Okay. Okay."

"And remember, if I'm the bad guy, none of this is real anyway. So, what's there to be worried about?" I rolled my eyes and walked past him through the open door into the lobby.

We hiked up like five or six flights of stairs, then into the dim halls of some kind of office. We walked past rows and rows of empty cubicles. No, not empty, they were still filled with the stuff of normal life. Birthday cards pinned to whiteboards, wrist pads to stop you from getting sprains from typing, photos of loved ones. One cube was decorated with streamers for someone's birthday. I stopped to touch a stuffed animal wearing a tiny shirt that said, 'Don't ask me, I only work here.' Its fur was covered in a fine layer of dust.

"C'mon, c'mon, it's right around the corner here," Ben said from ahead of me. I walked faster to catch up. He was standing in front of an office. It looked like every other office on every other floor of every other building in the world. He gestured for me to enter. There was a sign on the office door read, "Benjamin Hafler, Information Technologist."

He shooed me inside. "So... yeah," he said sheepishly. "This is my office. Or, I mean, this *was* my office. I lied to you, Elyse. I'm not a lawyer. I'm an IT guy. I was an IT guy."

The office was pretty boring. Modular furniture, a chair that looked more complicated than it needed to be. A computer. Some manuals and stacks of paper. I ran my hand over one binder and it came away covered in dust. There was a magic 8-ball and one of those clicky-clack things where a row of balls on strings bang into each other endlessly. There was a whiteboard that still had writing on it; a to-do list of things that would never get done. A window that looked out over the street below. A stock-photo poster of a nuclear mushroom cloud.

"You lied to me about being a lawyer?"

"I did," he admitted.

"Why?"

"I don't know," he said. I turned to look at him. He looked down at the floor. "I honestly don't know. Nervous I guess? Knee-jerk response. I was always a nerd. I remember being in college and telling girls I wanted to make video games for a living and they just shut down. So, I got in the habit of lying whenever I met someone hot. Lawyer, stockbroker, anesthesiologist. Whatever popped into my head at the moment. Nine times out of ten, I was going to strike out within a few minutes anyway, so I guess I didn't really worry about ever getting caught in the long term."

My eye caught a photo on his desk. It wasn't framed, it was just sort of propped up against the side of the computer. It was Ben, slightly younger and skinnier, and a plain-looking woman. His arm was around her. It was summertime. Behind me, Ben was still talking. "It's a silly thing to lie about now, but I just blurted it out the first time you asked. Then I was kinda stuck with the lie. I didn't want to admit that I lied to you, so I figured, who'd ever rat me out? But I know that you were sensing the lie, and, I don't know, maybe that was affecting how you saw me. So, I'm coming clean."

I picked up the photograph, "Who's this?"

"That's Colleen."

"Who is Colleen?"

"Someone who isn't alive anymore," he said in a tone that broke my heart.

I stared silently at the photo for a moment, then looked up at Ben. His eyes were turned away from me. "I didn't know," I said. "You never told me."

"You aren't the only one who's hurting. You aren't the only one who has experienced loss."

I put the photo back in its place. "I feel like I've been selfish."

"No. You just have more issues than me. You needed me to be strong. And actually, that helped. Being strong for you made me less focused on the things I've lost." I came around the desk and put my arms around him. "Since I'm coming clean, there's one more secret I want to show you. My office isn't the reason I keep coming back to Lake Clark. There isn't anything in my office that really calls to me. Do you want to see what I come here for? See my secret place?"

I remember coming to the realization there in his office that I had been too focused on me. Ben was right, I hadn't really ever asked him about who he was. I was so concerned with my own past, my own issues, my own demons, that I... I don't know, just assumed that he didn't have any of his own. Was that why I'd been fantasizing that he was some sort of evil, soulless maniac? I hadn't bothered to find out who Ben the human was. I was too busy thinking about him as Ben the savior, or Ben the teacher, or Ben the provider. Now, sure, he could have been a little more open about himself. But I guess I just assumed that was because he was scared or shy or too busy saving, teaching, and providing for me to ever really show his true self. "I want to know you," I said. "I want to know the real you... Even if you are a dork." I smiled to let him know I was joking.

"Okay. I'll take you to my 'inner sanctum'." Understand, that didn't sound nearly as ominous when he said it as when I'm saying it now. He even made little quote-marks with his hands. I slapped him on the butt and pushed him out of the office. We were both smiling.

Still Day 128:

Maybe I spoke too soon about it not sounding ominous. Later that day, I found myself standing in a completely pitch-black room. Ben had run off somewhere. I could hear him banging around in the darkness. I called out to him, "What are you doing? I can't see anything."

"Hold on, I'm trying to find the power switch on the generator."

"Are you sure this isn't dangerous? You promised this wouldn't be dangerous."

"The only dangerous thing was how I almost electrocuted myself when I hooked this generator in. Hold on. Almost got it." A few more banging sounds could be heard, and then a couple of curse words. Then one more bang.

The bar is suddenly filled with lights. Someone had strung Christmas lights all over the ceiling. Music floods the room. Ben came in from somewhere in the back. "So, welcome to the Lucky Lady."

"What is this place?" I said, looking around. This bar, with all the lights on, and the music on, it seemed... normal? Like, in the stores we'd looted, or the office we'd just left, or even the house where we found Detective Stubbs, everything seemed dead. Abandoned. But this place somehow still had that spark of life. Like you could expect a whole bunch of regulars to just walk in the door any minute.

"This is the bar I used to hang out at after work. Back when I had a job, you know?" He walked behind the bar and pulled two bottles of beer out from under the counter. I sat down at a bar stool and let him serve me. That dork even put a napkin down under the bottle.

"You drive all the way out here, spent all that time restoring this place, so you could just sit and drink alone?" I said, discretely trying to mop up some spilled foam.

"After everyone died, before I met you, I got really sad, you know? I mean of course you know; you went through the same thing. And I started to think about where I was happiest, and it was this bar, and I wanted to keep that... keep that small part of what I'd had."

We joked for a little bit, pretending everything was normal about the world. I got up and wandered around. Ben had carefully placed photographs and keepsakes of people at various tables. As I passed certain photos, Ben would call out a name and a little story about the person. Co-workers, college classmates, childhood friends, his whole life all in one room. Some of the tables even had empty glasses on them. It was like a memorial.

"It's not the same of course," he said. "The kegs all went flat, and the bottled beer is kinda skunky now." He took a sip of beer, put it back on the bar, and stuck out his tongue.

I realized that this place was his bottlecap collection. "Why didn't you tell me about it?"

"This is where I go when I can't take it anymore. When you're acting all crazy and I'm freaking out because I'm worried that the canned food has spoiled and I'm lonely and I miss my friends and miss drinking pitchers over the pinball machine talking about politics and movies and girls."

114

"You used to play pinball?" There were two machines against the wall, blinking and bright.

"I didn't 'play' pinball. That implies it was a game. I was an 'artist.'"

"Oh really?"

"Really. And I'm not even lying about that."

I walked over to one of the machines and put my hand on the buttons. "You know, I'm not so bad at pinball myself," I said. I bumped into the cabinet with my hip, playfully.

He came around from behind the bar, carrying two more beers. "You don't say?"

"I do say. I used to work as a lifeguard when I was in high school. Had a crush on some of the boys, and you'd always find them at the machine in the snack bar."

Ben put the beers on a nearby table. He picked up a box of coins and offered it to me. "You know, I happen to have some quarters, if you'd like to test your metal...."

"You're on, 'Mr. Hafler'."

I don't remember who won the game. I do remember lights and sounds and the two of us laughing, and me even trying to pinch Ben's butt to make him mess up. I remember the first game ended with a kiss, and an embrace. As did the second, and the third. I remember several beers that weren't nearly as flat as Ben had apologized about. I remember feeling normal that day. I'd been happy other days, and I'd been sad other days. I'd been relaxed and free, and I'd been anxious and having meltdowns. But this was the first time since I'd woken up sick in my apartment that morning that things felt *normal*. It was a good feeling. Not going to lie.

My beer had run out. "I am going to get another one," I said to Ben. "Can I interest you?"

He didn't look up. "Don't distract me, woman; I'm in range of a high score!" he said in mock anger. I crossed the room, stopping briefly in front of some tables to pay respects to the photos of all those people I didn't know. I went behind the bar and took another beer. "Multiball!" Ben cried out from across the room. Lights and sounds and popping noises. I think now that the pinball machine might have even had a police siren on top, spinning and a-wooga-ing.

I saw my reflection in the mirror behind the bar. I looked healthy. Behind me Ben played in the distance. He turned around and glanced in my direction, smiling sweetly at the back of my head from across the room.

I opened the bottle and the cap went rolling across the countertop. I chased after it so I could throw it away. It came to rest against an old newspaper someone had left lying there. It was starting to fade and yellow. I read the headline. Immediately, everything went numb around me.

"Goddamn it. Your turn." Ben's voice sounded like he was talking from the other end of a long tunnel. I felt dizzy. I assume he saw me standing there, looking down at the paper and not responding. "Elyse, are you okay?" I didn't see him come over, but all of a sudden I felt his hand on my shoulder. "Elyse?" he said into my ear. I just pointed at the headline. It said, "Local Police Officer killed in drug raid," with a photo next to it. A photo of Hector.

Ben put his arms around me and rested his chin on my shoulder. He glanced at the article. "You look white as a sheet. Did you know him?"

"That's my brother," I said flatly.

"You never told me he was dead. I mean, I assumed that he died in the plague with everyone else."

"He... I...," I was confused. "I don't remember him dying. He wasn't dead. I would have remembered...." Was this right?

"Look at the date of this paper, it's two days before the plague really hit." Ben said. "Maybe you were already sick. Maybe you were so ill that it screwed with your memory."

"I think I would have remembered my own brother's death." I would have, right?

Ben spun me around and locked his gaze into mine. "Elyse, that bug really sucked. Do you remember what you were doing right before you got sick? Because I don't. Not really anyway. I was at work, and then everything gets all hazy and fever-dream and I woke up and it was a week later. If that happened to me, it happened to you, too."

I could feel tears welling up. Ben started getting blurry. "I don't remember anything. How could I have forgotten my own brother dying? Maybe that's why I've been thinking of him so much?"

"That could be. Some subconscious something maybe?" he wiped a tear from my cheek with a bar napkin.

"A nagging feeling about something I've forgotten...."

"I can't say that doesn't make sense," he said, tenderly.

"I've had this nagging feeling about something I've forgotten for months now. Something isn't right." What else had I forgotten? My life before was just fading away. Sand through my fingers. What did my mother look like? What was my best friend's name? I was sure I knew those things, but everything seemed just out of reach, just on the tip of my tongue.

"Maybe this was the thing that's subconsciously been holding you back. Maybe it's time to move on. Maybe it's time to completely let go of the past, and all those things in the past that aren't here anymore."

"There's so much that isn't here anymore." Ben had kept his past alive by using this bar and all these photos. But it was what, almost a year now? Almost a year since I'd spoken to anyone else; anyone that wasn't Ben or a hallucination of my dead brother. Was I holding on to the past? If so, why? It was gone, like a movie after the credits had rolled. All the characters in my life had said their last lines and left the stage. All except....

"Well, obviously the past isn't here anymore," said Ben. "But that's true of anybody's life anytime. There's always stuff from the past that we miss. But look around at what we do have." He gestured around and put on a smile. "The cabin, our little farm, afternoons on the riverbank, unlimited quarters for pinball. Each other." Was his smile real, or was he just trying to make me feel better? And did that even matter?

"Ben, I don't know if I could be here without you. You are my meaning and my reason for going on." I buried my face into his chest. He held me for what seemed like minutes. When he pulled back, there were two wet spots on his shirt where my eyes had been.

"Elyse, I've been waiting for the right time for this, and I know it doesn't mean much, but will you marry me?"

"Ben, I..."

He pulled a small box from out of his jacket. The lid sprung open. Inside was a gigantic diamond. "Okay, I can't take credit for the size, because I didn't technically 'pay' for it. But I did scrounge it from the nicest jewelry store I could find. And I know it's not legal or anything without a preacher, but I know I'm already the last man on earth, will you make me the luckiest?" I think he might have even gotten down on one knee.

"Will you tell me about Colleen?" I asked.

"I will... someday. Not today, but someday."

"Do you miss her?"

"I miss everything about the old world, sweetie, but there's no point in missing what's never coming back. All we have now is each other. And this beautiful, quiet Earth we have all to ourselves. We need to look forward; both of us. If we don't, the past is going to consume us."

I took the ring out of the box and put it on my finger. I took Ben's hand in mine and held it tight. Squeezed it hard. Squeezed it like if I lost it, if I let go, I'd fall and fall and fall into... I don't know.

"To the future!" I finally said to him. There was a smile on my face, but I'm not sure if it was because I was happy, or if I was just trying to make myself feel happy.

Day 192:

The months went quickly after that cathartic afternoon at the bar. We never did have a formal ceremony or anything like that. Never stood under a tree and said vows or got wedding photos. But I wore the ring every day. Well, until I lost it in the garden somewhere. But Ben got me another one soon after. And we acted like we were married. And I was happy.

I don't remember exactly how long it had been because every day was pretty much like the last. "There are no weekends in the apocalypse," Ben once said. There were no alarm clocks waking us up or meetings to not be late for. No birthdays or appointments to remember. The only thing that made one memory different from another was the season. And I definitely remember that it was fall then. The vegetables in the garden were full grown and ripe and ready to be picked.

Ben was wherever it was that Ben goes. I was lying on the grass, looking up at the sky. Watching the clouds fly by overhead. Are clouds like snowflakes? Is every single one different? I mean, I assume they are, but you always hear people talking about snowflakes, and yet no one says 'unique as a cloud.' Maybe there are only a few kinds of clouds that pass by again and again? Maybe no one ever took the time to watch them long enough to know. I had all the time in the world.

I already described what it was like when Hector arrives. Sounds sounding backwards, that static electricity. Were the clouds moving backwards that day? They usually came from one direction, but now they seemed to be coming from another. That sudden awareness that my stomach hurt, and that it had been hurting for a while. I sat up. I turned around, and behind me was a shadow. No, not a shadow. More like a blind spot. A glitch that looked like something moving out of the corner of your eye, even when you were staring directly at it. I froze. It was trying to move closer. Trying to come into focus. I broke into a run towards my backpack.

"Elyse!" Hector shouted.

I rummaged through my bag, and pulled out a bottle of the pills Ben gave me. The ones that kept me pretty much sane since the last time I'd seen Hector. "You aren't real!" I waved the bottle at him like it was a knife.

"I'm real," Hector said calmly. "Well, as real as anything here is."

"You're dead. You're just a ghost." I struggled with the bottle. Even after the apocalypse they still had child-proof caps. "What are you...?" I got it open and poured pills into my mouth. They tasted bitter as I chewed them defiantly. "That's not going to do anything. Those aren't actual pills. They are just the dream of pills."

"I'll overdose," I warned him.

Hector chuckled. "You can't overdose on imaginary medicine." I gagged and spit out the pills. I threw the empty bottle at him.

"What do you want? How do I make you go away?"

"We found the storage shed. On the highway outside of Lake Clark." The storage shed. The place where my body....

"There is no storage shed in Lake Clark!" I screamed. Then more quietly, "I went to Lake Clark. It was just his office." Then barely a whisper, "...and a bar."

"You didn't go to Lake Clark. You went to a simulation of what you remember Lake Clark looking like."

"You are just a hallucination. I've been reading up on psychiatry. You are just a delusion because of my overwhelming sense of survivor's guilt combined with my general psychotic tendencies." I was quoting.

"Read up on psychiatry?" He chuckled. "Who do you think wrote those textbooks? They are just data files being downloaded into your brain. They say whatever it is that Benjamin wants them to say. Just like he fed you that fake newspaper article about me."

"He wouldn't do that. He's not like that," I pleaded. Real Hector didn't know Ben. And fake hallucination Hector definitely didn't know Ben.

"He's done it before," Hector said flatly. "We fished her body out of a drainage ditch just around the time he took you."

"Colleen?"

"You know her?"

I paused. "He said she was his ex-girlfriend. That she died in the plague."

"Kinda chubby? Mousy-brown hair? He actually showed her to you?" he said, incredulously.

"He had her photo on his desk. In his office in Lake Clark." The girl in the photo....

"Dammit. He's getting bolder. He knows we can't find him. He's baiting us. Do you remember, the last time I was here, everything stopped all of a sudden?"

"I blacked out. From the stress."

"You didn't black out. He panicked and turned off the simulation. Everything just 'disconnected.' We rushed off to look for the storage unit and we found it, right outside of Lake Clark like you said it would be. But by the time we got there, he'd cleared it out. He took you and the computers and everything and he left. We don't know where."

"If you're real, why did you abandon me here? It's been months."

"While the simulation was down he increased his encryption. It's been impossible to hack in until now. We've only just figured out how to reach you again. And he's got alarms set up everywhere now. I'm not sure we'll be able to get back in any more after today."

I remembered what Hector had told me to look for. "He hasn't let anything slip." I said. "I've been listening, but he hasn't said anything." Had I really been listening though? I didn't remember anything suspicious coming from Ben's mouth since the time he mentioned Lake Clark. But after his innocent explanation and the proposal, I guess I was, I don't know, too lovestruck to really be paying attention? Maybe I didn't want to hear anything that would break the spell. Was it my fault? Was I just being naïve?

"No. He's not that careless. He made that mistake once and we almost caught him. He's not going to make a mistake like that again. We're still looking for you, but I don't know if we'll find you in time."

"In time...?"

"This place isn't stable. It might not look like it now, but I know you can feel that more and more things aren't quite right. Strange shadows. Weird, garbled voices just out of range. The software he's using was made for games people would play for an hour at a time. It wasn't designed to be left on indefinitely. And the longer the simulation runs, the more each little error is compounded. Soon nothing here is going to be making sense. And when you stop making sense and he can't use this little playground for his amusement anymore, what do you think he's going to do to you?" Drainage ditch.

I flopped down onto the ground. "Why can't you just let me be happy?" Why couldn't things just be normal for once? Why does everything keep falling apart? I thought I'd found some meaning and purpose in this world, but if it's really unreal then...

Hector knelt beside me. "Because the clock is ticking," he said. "It's not like you can stay here in this little world, even if you wanted to. It's going to end one way or another. The simulation will crash, or Benjamin will get bored with you and just strangle you while you lie there helpless."

"I don't know what else I can do. Every day I try so hard to keep it together. I'm trying to keep it together. I'm trying not to feel trapped. I'm trying not to feel like there's no point anymore because everyone is dead. I'm trying to deal with the guilt of being alive." I was just trying to make sense of this absurd universe. I was just trying to figure out the rules of this place. The rules of being alive and how to feel and what to do. But everything kept changing. The ground kept falling out from under me. As soon as I thought I had it under control, I didn't. What should I do?

"There is one other option. It should work, but you are going to have to trust me."

I remember saying, "I trust *Hector*..."

"But you aren't sure if I'm really Hector. Yeah, I got it. But you are going to have to work through that and start helping me help you. You have to put your faith in the world beyond this one. There is a way to

124

shock your brain out of the simulation. To wake yourself up."

"How?"

"You have to die, Elyse," he said.

I blinked at Hector, "What?!?"

"Don't panic. If you die here, like if you jump off a bridge or something, the simulation will automatically end and you'll wake up. You'll leave this absurd world where nothing makes sense and wake up in the place that matters."

"But if I die in the computer, don't I also die in the real world?"

Hector sighed. "This isn't a cheesy sci-fi movie. This place you are in, it is like a dream. If you dream you are falling, what happens right before you hit the ground?"

"You wake up."

Hector nodded. "Yes, yes, exactly. You wake up. And once you wake up, maybe you can unhook yourself from the machine and run away. Maybe you can scream for help and someone will hear you. Maybe you can pick up something heavy and bean him when he opens the door to check on you. But at least you'll have a chance. If you stay here much longer, you won't."

"I don't know if I can."

"You did it before. Remember the time I found you half-conscious on the floor covered in pills and vomit?"

I did remember. I didn't want to, but I did. "I didn't want to live then. I want to live now."

"Dying is living. All you have to do is jump. Take that leap. You can do it."

"I don't know. I don't..."

125

All of a sudden I heard a car engine in the distance. Ben. I turned to look and saw him coming down the driveway. I turned back around, but Hector was gone. Just completely... gone.

I must have still been confused when Ben opened the car door. Was I still talking? Was I calling out for Hector? "Elyse? Are you talking to someone?" Ben said as he approached.

"I... I was just humming a tune."

"Are you okay? You look spooked." He seemed genuinely concerned. But was that an act? Was everything he'd said to me these past few months an act? I touched the large diamond ring around my finger. Was it unreal? It felt solid. Everything here felt solid. Everything here felt soiled.

I lied again, "I'm just feeling a little sick, I guess. Maybe a cold or a chill." I faked a smile so he wouldn't worry.

"Well, let's get you inside. I'll put on some hot cocoa." Ben put his arm around my shoulders and guided me inside. As we walked, I scanned the horizon, looking for any sign that Hector had ever been here at all, but there was none.

Day 200:

Was it real? Was Hector real? Was this universe real? Was I real? If I was real, and this place was real, then there were rules I could figure out. I'd know what to do. If this place wasn't real, and that other world was real, I'd know what to do and there would be rules I could figure out. But those rules would be different, wouldn't they? They'd have to be. Ben is a good guy. Ben is a bad guy. See? The rules are different. But how to know?

The words Hector said kept with me in the days after I saw him. *Strange shadows. Weird, garbled voices just out of range....* Was that shadow strange? No, it was just a branch, blowing in the wind. Was that a voice? No, it was just the river. Was that bird staring at me? Listening to me? Talking to me? Every bird looks alike, right? I mean, just because you see a bird in one place and then again in another place, doesn't mean it's the same bird. Lots of birds look like that. Lots of birds stare at me as I'm walking in the woods. Were they agents of Ben, spying on me? Were they agents of Hector, protecting me? Was it my own imagination? Was it psychosis? Was it just a god-damn bird and stop being so dramatic, Elyse, you are driving yourself crazy.

I was walking in the woods that day, like maybe a week after Hector told me that I needed to kill myself. Maybe I figured that if I explored the forest enough, I would be sure that this was real. And it was. Or it seemed to be. The forest went on and on and I kept looking for trees or rocks that looked out of place or not quite finished and everything seemed normal. And Stubbs was with me, getting into whatever smelly thing he could find to get into and sniffing at every tree and rock along the way.

And I was walking and I was thinking that if Stubbs couldn't tell anything was wrong, that maybe nothing was wrong. Maybe all those shadows and noises were nothing more than my imagination. I should just trust Stubbs instead of my own stupid brain. I let the dog lead me; just following him along through the forest. He ran ahead. I jogged a little to catch up. I remember calling out, but he was getting further and further from me. Was he just happy to be free? Did he see something up ahead? Was he being called? He was almost out of range. I could barely make him out between the trees, darting to and fro.

The path turned to the right, around a big boulder that was covered in moss. As I walked past it, a flash of color filled my eyes. I blinked several times, and Hector was there, leaning against the rock. I frowned, but maintained. I didn't say anything. Ignore him, Elyse. Just a dream. He'll go away. Focus. Dog. Find my dog. I walked faster, deliberately. "Stubbs." I called out.

The path turned again and again. Left, right, left, right. Around trees and big rocks and even an old, rusted car that somehow somebody had left here years ago. And behind every one of these things, Hector; just leaning quietly, waiting for me to react to him. He was never moving or trying to catch up as I walked past him, he just was always, somehow, in front of me; waiting behind the next blind.

"I still can't believe that you are anything more than a hallucination," I finally said as I walked past him for what must have been the tenth time. I didn't even look in his direction.

He started walking behind me, keeping his distance, but now actively following me. Was it because I'd acknowledged him? "Is that what you actually think or just what you want to think?" he said.

I turned to face him. "Would the real Hector keep torturing me like this?"

"Would the real Hector ever give up on you?" he pleaded. "Would the real Hector stop fighting to save you? Every day, over and over again, fighting to save you?"

"You want me to kill myself."

"I don't want you to kill yourself. I want you to save yourself. You aren't actually dying, you'll be *ascending*. It's not a real suicide, you are just shocking the system in order to end the simulation. Then you wake up. I want you to be okay... to be safe." He moved closer and closer to me. Like he wanted to take me in his arms.

"And if you are wrong?" I asked.

"I'm not wrong."

"But what if you were? What if you are just in my head?"

Hector paused and gathered his thoughts. "Okay, what *if* I am just a delusion? Do you really want to live here anyway? There's nothing left. There's no future. Nothing matters here. It's just you and some creepy nerd living among the ruins; getting older and sicker and eventually dying pointless deaths anyway. Wouldn't it be best to just end it now?"

"But we won't be alone," I said, challenging him. "We're going to have a baby."

Hector looked up at the sky. His face contorted. "What? A virtual baby? That's so fucking insane!" he shouted at me. His fists were balled.

"What's insane about that?"

"You can't have a baby, Elyse. It wouldn't be real. It'd be..."

"It would be as real as you are."

Hector bit his lip in frustration. "You've got to listen to me. I'm begging you, Elyse. You have to get out of here. I have to save you. How can I convince you?"

"How are you even here anyway? If this is all what you say, and there's a computer in a dungeon somewhere, how are you 'hacking in?' It doesn't make any sense that it would be connected to the internet at all, right?" I mean, I don't know much about computers, but that's how I think they work.

"It's got something to do with processing capacity," Hector said. "You can't run a simulation like this on a laptop. He's using the cloud or something. I don't know. I'm just the person talking to you, I'm not the tech nerds who did the hacking. We have a whole team of people working on your case."

"Just leave me alone," I said firmly, "I'm happy here." I turned and started down the path again. Stubbs, where the hell was Stubbs? I didn't have time to deal with Hector, whether real or imagined, I needed to focus on the present. I needed to get out of these woods before I was hopelessly lost. I needed to find my dog. I needed to....

Hector again appeared in front of me. It wasn't like he teleported; it was like he'd always been there, right in front of me.

"I said leave me alone!" I cried. I ran past him. Faster. Run away. Run away from the craziness. Run away from my own dumb brain. Can a person run faster than a thought? Hector was in front of me again. I was turned around. Stubbs? Was I lost? Did I backtrack?

"I can't leave you alone," he pleaded. "I need to save you. Why won't you let me save you?"

Save me. I needed someone to save me. "I can't afford you anymore. I can't afford the comfort of hallucinations and daydreams. I have to be here; I have to be strong." Would Ben save me?

Hector's voice started to crack with frustration. "We don't have much time left. Every time we find a new backdoor into the simulation, he closes it. At some point, we'll be out of options."

"Good." I cursed.

"Elyse, you aren't taking your meds in the real world. Every day your brain is getting more and more scrambled by this simulator. Soon you'll be completely gone. You won't know what's real anymore. You won't be functional. And then it'll be too late."

I started running. I pushed through the brush on the side of the trail and entered the deep forest. But Hector's voice was right beside me. I couldn't see him anymore, but his voice still sounded like he was right by my ear... right inside my skull.

"If you won't listen to me," Hector's voice said, "maybe you'll listen to mom. She's been so worried about you she just sits here in the precinct, day after day, waiting for a sign from you."

Mom?

I heard a disembodied voice coming from somewhere above me, like an angel's, "Elly, it's me. You have to come back to us. Please...."

No.

I ran through the woods. I remember falling down, tripping over an unseen root. My hands were sticky, but was it mud or blood? I stumbled to my feet and kept running. "Baby, please come back to us," Mom said.

Another voice this time, younger, "Honey, we need you." Sara? That sounded like my friend Sara.

"Aunt Elyse, remember me?" said a child.

"Elyse, this is Doctor Butler. It's okay to be scared." His voice was authoritative. It made me stop in my tracks... but just for a second. Got to keep running. Get out of the forest. Get away from the voices in your head. Which way was out? Where'd my dog go? If I could just find my dog....

Hector again appeared out of nowhere. He was wearing his detective's badge on a chain around his neck. "We're all here, Sis," he said. "We are all trying to help you."

I covered my head with my hands and blindly tried to tackle him. But either I missed, or I passed right through him like a ghost. I was on the ground again. I got to my feet. My hair had weeds and dirt in it. Run.

"I made you a card for your birthday," said the boy.

"Elly, honey. You missed your birthday, but we still had a party for you. The presents are wrapped and waiting." Mom?

Another voice joined the chorus. "This is Dan, we worked on that commercial together a few months ago. Remember?" Where were the voices coming from? I spun around, but no one was there, Hector wasn't there. Behind a tree? Behind all the trees?

Doctor Butler said calmly, "We've built up a lot of trust over the years you and I, Elyse. You know I'm telling you things for your own good."

132

Sara: "I miss the lunches and happy hours we spent together." Stop. Please.

Dan: "If you wake up, I'd like to take you on a date." No. Stop.

Mom: "Elly, please. You've got to wake up!" No. leave me alone.

Sara: "If you don't come back, who am I going to gossip about pervy casting directors with?" Run.

Mom: "I know it's scary, honey. But you've got to jump." Jump?

Doctor: "I wish there was another way."

The voices were coming from all sides now. They were everywhere. They were nowhere. "You can do it, Aunt Elyse," said the boy.

"It's not so hard. Just let go."

"It's the only way."

"We'll save you but you've got to take that first step."

"Jump."

"Jump."

"Jump!"

"Jump!"

Hector appeared right in front of me. "Jump," he said. "We'll catch you."

I felt dizzy. Was I spinning around? Was the world spinning around me? I swung my fists blindly. "Leave me alone!" I screamed, "All of you leave me alone!"

"Jump! Jump! Jump! Jump!" chanted the chorus of disembodied voices, all in unison. I tried to start running, but it was like that children's game where they spin you around over and over and watch you try to walk a straight line. I fell to the ground. I must have hit my head. Everything went blank as the voices suddenly stopped.

The next thing I heard was Ben's voice from off in the distance. "Elyse? Are you still out there on your walk?" he was shouting. Looking for me.

I opened my eyes. The sunlight streamed through the trees and the leaves shook in the breeze. A small cloud passed overhead. I sat up. I was panting for breath. My clothes were covered in dirt and grass stains. The palms of my hands stung. Stubbs was sitting next to me, chewing on a stick without a care in the world.

"Yeah. Just lying here in the sun." I shouted to Ben. "Enjoying nature and all that. Think I fell asleep for a second." I looked around, but there was no sign of Hector. There was no sign of Mom or anybody else. I stood up. The trail seemed straighter now. I knew the way home again.

Day 202:

Nighttime. There's enough light to see the ceiling. Full moon, I guess? Could the stars be bright enough to light the room like this? If this is unreal, then why couldn't they be bright enough? These aren't my real eyes; they can see anything Ben wants me to see. Does he want me to look at him while he sleeps? Is that even Ben in that body breathing quietly beside me? Maybe he's disconnected, wandering around in the real world. Would he wake if I shook him?

Ben rolled over and draped his arm across my waist. Was he listening to my thoughts? No, that seems silly. But then again, if nothing is real, anything is possible, right? I continue staring at the ceiling. When I was a kid, I put star shaped glow-in-the-dark stickers on the ceiling of my bedroom. I used to look up at them and pretend they were real stars. But they weren't real stars, they were just a simulation. If I could peel the roof off this room and see the sky, would I be looking at real stars then? Or just fake stars pasted onto the ceiling of this world that Ben created?

I could feel Ben open his eyes. I could hear his breathing change. "Can't sleep?" he said groggily.

I didn't turn to face him. "I'm fine." I said flatly. I didn't want him touching me right now.

"Are you okay?" he asked.

"I'm fine," I repeated.

Ben sat up and put his face in my line of sight. "I'm worried about you."

"There's nothing to worry about." I didn't even pout. I was just numb. If this wasn't real, then what could go wrong, right? You can't actually get hurt while playing a video game.

"I think maybe you've been taking too many of those pills. They aren't candy."

"I'm taking exactly as many as I need to take."

Ben sighed, skeptically. "I trust you. But you'd tell me if there was anything wrong, right?"

"Of course, why wouldn't I?" Wouldn't I?

"Because you don't want me to worry about you," Ben said sleepily.

"Ben, we both know you'll always be worried about me." That much was true.

"Fine. I won't worry. But I trust you'll let me know if any of your symptoms start getting worse."

I finally turned to face him. "Of course. Get some sleep," I said. I smiled sweetly. Was it a fake smile? Was it even possible to have a real smile on a fake face?

Ben patted my tummy and rolled over again. "I love you," he said softly.

"I know," I replied.

Very soon after, Ben's breathing got heavy again, as he fell back into a deep sleep. I blinked twice and continued to sleeplessly stare up at the ceiling. I raised my hand in the air and gestured at a mirror that hung on the wall. If this was a simulation, if this were some kind of video game I was controlling with my mind, then everything is possible? Right? Shouldn't I have superpowers? I willed the mirror to fall off the wall. If it's my world, why can't I make things happen? The mirror didn't budge an inch. It gave me no sign that I had any control over how the world worked. I felt powerless.

The disembodied voices continued their chant in my head, as they'd done since I saw Hector in the woods. Sometimes loudly, sometimes so softly that you weren't sure you could hear them at all, but constant. "Jump. Jump. Jump!" they called, "Jump! Do it. Do it. It's the only way. Jump. Do it. Jump! Jump! Jump! Jump!"

Day 205:

I remember I was sitting on the porch. It must have been a few days after the incident in the woods. My hands were still a little scraped up. I was sitting in one of the rockers that Ben had salvaged from somewhere. It wasn't bright that day, even though I don't remember there being any clouds. Everything had a greyish clarity to it. I think that there was tea on the table, or cookies, or maybe a whole uneaten breakfast. I don't know. But I remember that Ben was there, trying to play a guitar. He'd gotten an instruction book and learned some chords. He wasn't good. But in a way, it was completely adorable. Definitely the sort of thing that would have made me fall in love with him a few months ago. But now? Was he being fake, was he being real? Was he playing the guitar poorly in front of me because he wanted to entertain me, to trick me, or actually because he wanted to keep his mind busy? I don't know.

I think he was talking to me, but I honestly don't remember what he was saying. I don't think I was listening. I was just staring off into space over his shoulder. At the far end of the porch, Hector was standing a quiet vigil, now wearing his police uniform. He wasn't saying anything, or even moving, he was just looking at me, watching me intensely. Silently pleading with me to end things with Ben and come back to the real world. But *this* was the real world, wasn't it? I don't even know anymore.

Hector, if you are just a delusion, you could at least try a little harder.

Day 209:

It's not to say I was completely dysfunctional by that time. I know that the cliché is that once someone starts down a path of mental illness, they just spiral and spiral and it's 100% bad days. But real brains don't work like that, even if they are broken. I was still tending to my garden. Still playing fetch with my dog. Still eating... sometimes. My vegetables had gotten ripe by that time. I looked out the garden from the kitchen window. I remembered when I planted them, how excited I was to show off for Ben. How excited I had been to contribute to our little family, our little world.

I put on some clothes and took a basket. It was foggy that day, everything was covered with tiny droplets of dew. I put on boots. I stood on the porch for a long time, trying to feel the wetness of the railing on my hand. Did I feel water, or did I just *think* I felt water? I closed my eyes and tried again. I guess it felt wet. But could I trust my own nerve endings to tell me the truth? If this was just a dream, wouldn't it feel the same way?

I opened my eyes and scanned the horizon. Everything out there was still. Quiet. Dead. I think Ben was around somewhere, but I don't remember exactly where he was. He was obviously trying to give me space and stay out of my way. I felt alone. I wished that a plane would pass by. I strained to hear a voice shouting in the distance, but there wasn't one. If someone else showed up, wouldn't that mean that this was the real world after all?

139

Someone besides Hector, I mean. Hector was always there. Sometimes right in front of me. Sometimes only out of the corner of my eye. Sometimes invisible, but somehow still nearby. His color was often wrong now. He'd be black and white, or completely mauve, or glowing. He'd be the wrong size, or shape, or he'd move in a stutter-step like one of those old film projectors that kept skipping frames.

Sometimes Hector would try to talk. But more often than not, his voice was garbled and distorted, like a mistuned radio that wasn't picking up the right frequency. That morning I just tried to ignore him, the way I'd been ignoring him for weeks now.

I started picking ripe tomatoes and putting them in the basket. I grabbed the biggest, juiciest one on the vine. Hector screamed in a way that startled me. When I looked down again I could see that the tomato in my hand was rotten and covered in worms. I dropped it in disgust and ran inside, in tears.

Day 211:

I was so hot and cold with Ben during that time. Some days, I missed him and needed him more than anything else in the world. Other times, I couldn't stand to be in his presence at all. What was real? What wasn't real? One could only trust one's own senses. If my eyes and ears were telling me this world was real, why was my heart telling me it wasn't? And what is 'real' anyway? If you believe in god and you know that there is a heaven above us, outside of the earth, then is the earth real? Or is it just an illusion that stops us from seeing the heaven that is all around us? And if Hector is right, and this world I see is just a computer, and the world I knew before is out there somewhere, maybe that's like heaven, right? And you can never know if heaven is real or not real because it's not something you can see. You have to wait until the real world ends. And that only happens when you die. You have to commit, you have to leave this place forever to get to the next place, and everybody says that the next place is better. The priests say the next place is better, Hector says the next place is better, all those television shows and books and pop culture all try to convince me the next place is better.

But okay, if that's true, why didn't everybody just kill themselves? (I mean before everybody died of that virus). Pretty much nobody was going around killing themselves to get to heaven. Why is that? Is it because they weren't sure? Is it because despite all the churches and priests and movies and bibles and everything, they still were worried that this life, as bad as it could be, was just all there is. Nobody kills themselves to get to the next world. They just muddle through this world as best they can and figure they'll find out eventually. Fuck you, Hector. Why should I listen to you? You think you are some kind of angel that comes down to earth to show us mortals the path. But you just confuse. If Hector was so smart, he'd just find me and wake me up, or turn the computer program off or something. He'd *do* something, not just tell me to do something. He's like a street-preacher yelling at passersby to repent. He doesn't have proof, can't show you anything. He just asks you to have faith and believe.

Do I have faith? I guess I had faith in the Hector I knew before everybody died. This Hector though... It is really him? I wish there was some way he could convince me it was really him. But he can't, because anything he could say would just be something my dumb, broken brain could also just be saying to itself. He could tell me all sorts of things about what the real, real world was like and it wouldn't matter because it could just be me making it up.

Do I have faith in Ben? I... I don't know. He seems sincere, but that's just how an evil genius would seem, right? Maybe I'm being paranoid. I wish there was some way he could convince me it was really him. But he can't convince me because if he's right, if this is the real world and not a computer game, he can no more prove that than an atheist could prove that heaven doesn't really exist. How do you know what is real and what isn't real? Damn, I'm going in circles.

We were lying in bed that night. I was staring at the ceiling again. It looked real. If I reached my hand up high enough it would feel real. But does that make it real? And even if it wasn't real, would that matter? We are all trapped in the prison of our own brains, looking out at the world through the windows of our eyes. What I see *is* what's real, just because that's the thing I see. I don't know how else to explain it.

I look over and Ben is awake, staring at me as I'm lost in thought. He's smiling sweetly. I roll over to avoid his gaze.

Day 214:

The voices were back. They came and went, sometimes louder, sometimes so soft you couldn't hear them. Sometimes they went on for hours, sometimes it was just a single scream. The pills helped. But a person could only take so many pills.

That day, all together, a chorus had been chanting, "Jump. Jump. We'll catch you!" since I woke up. I remember clearly. I was sitting on the porch, wrapped in a blanket, probably looking exhausted from lack of sleep. Hair tied in knots. Some vomit still on my shirt from when I threw up all those pills. The doctors warned me not to take too many. Or was that the voices? Either way, they were right. My stomach was not good.

Ben was sitting beside me. Our dog napping blissfully by his feet. He was reading another psychiatry textbook, I think. I heard my mom's voice say, "You have to wake up."

"Mom?" I whispered.

"What did you say, honey?" said Ben. I just waved him off with my hand. "Oh, okay. I thought you said something." He went back to reading.

Hector said, "...strange shadows. Weird, garbled voices just out of range...." Or maybe he didn't say it. Maybe I was just remembering him saying it from before.

"Elly, you have to wake up," said my mom. "There's only one way to wake up."

Hector's voice told me, "the longer the simulation runs, the more each little error is compounded. Soon, nothing here is going to be making

144

sense." From behind him the chorus chanted, "It's all a dream. Jump. Jump. Jump...."

"The longer the simulation runs, the more each little error is compounded. Soon nothing here is going to be making sense," I must have repeated out loud.

Ben put down his book and leaned toward me. "How are you doing Elly?" he said sweetly.

My blood ran cold. "You called me Elly."

"So?"

It seemed so obvious now. "You've never called me Elly before. Only my mom calls me Elly. My mom just called me Elly, in my head. Are you listening to my head, Ben?"

It was a simple question. Ben just stared at me, blankly. He closed his eyes for a second, as if he was about to say something. But then he stood up and threw the book he was holding into the garden. He screamed at the sky. It was unlike him. If I thought he was being honest, I would have felt bad for upsetting him. But you can't feel bad about something unreal. It's just fiction. This world is just a character I play on stage. Ben isn't Ben. I'm not me.

He regained his composure and turned back around to me, "I don't know what to do," he said.

"I used to be happy here," I replied.

"I don't know what's wrong with you."

"I mean, it was crazy at first, but things were so nice in our little cabin. No stress. I just wish it was real. I just wish it meant something." Part of me *did* wish it was real. Most of me, if I'm being honest. I know, that sounds crazy right? Wanting the end of the world? But it was so easy and comforting here. Like being snuggled in your mom's arms when you were a baby, or being huddled up under a blanket by a fire with some cocoa

145

and a good book. Was that what made it so hard to leave? Was that what made it so hard to believe that this place wasn't real? Did I deserve a happily ever after?

"I can't become a therapist." Ben said. "All I can do is give you more pills."

"There are no pills, Ben. They are just pixels."

Ben continued to plead with me. "How can I make you believe this is the real world? How can I make you come back to me?"

"Why don't you let me go, Ben? Are you going to keep me in here forever?" Was there any point in asking?

Ben kneeled down in front of me and turned my head with his hands so he could look me directly in the eye. "I'm not keeping you here, Elyse. Where else would you go? There's nowhere else to go."

"I could go back to the real world. I could pet a real dog. Not just a simulation dog." Everything here was cold. Everything here was just a shadow of something real, something just out of reach that I couldn't see.

"Detective Stubbs is a real dog," Ben said. He turned and spoke to the dog, "Isn't that right, D.S.?" The dog didn't answer.

"I could read real books. I could listen to real records. I could eat real chocolate." I said aloud.

I'm not sure I could even really hear Ben anymore. Everything was fading out, going grey. Like the image on an old television that just fades out after you turn it off. "Maybe that'll help...," I think he was saying. "Baby, here's what I'm going to do. I'm going to go pick you some strawberries."

"All I have to do is let go. That's what Hector keeps saying."

146

A voice from outside my head said, "Remember when I first found you, and you were on that bridge? I gave you some strawberries I had in my bag? That seemed to cheer you up."

"Hector says all I need to do is jump and he'll catch me in the real world," I replied.

"Can I trust you to not do anything crazy until I get back?" I took a sip of the tea that Ben had prepared. It was cold and tasteless. I stared off into the garden. There was a book there, pages spread apart, spine broken, lying amongst the cucumbers. It seemed out of place there. "Hmm," said Ben, who had been waiting for a reply. "I'll take that as a yes. I'll be back as soon as I can, okay, baby?'" He kissed me on the forehead and then disappeared from my view.

The chorus of voices appeared to take his place. "Jump. Jump. Jump," they chanted softly. Hector was in the garden, in his policeman's dress uniform, looking crisp and clean. He stared down at the book carelessly left on the ground. Then he looked directly at me.

"Jump," he said.

I couldn't leave. Not yet. "Ben says I have to wait here. He says he has strawberries for me. He says they are real strawberries."

"We're out of time."

I remember being confused when he said that. "We have all the time in the world, Hector. Nothing here is real. Time isn't even real. Not in here."

"We were able to pull some of the prototype code he's using to run this simulation off a hard drive we recovered from his house. There was a program in there codenamed 'strawberry.'"

"Ben is going to give me strawberries."

"This program, it's designed to stabilize the simulation for long-term use. But a side effect is that it'll rewire your brain. It'll lobotomize you. He's going to boot up that program, and that's it. No more Elyse. You've got to get out of here now."

"Why should I believe you?" I asked.

"I don't know what I can do to convince you," said Hector. "I could tell you some stories about when we were kids, or what your old apartment looked like, or describe the ridiculous haircut on that loser you went to senior prom with. But if you think I'm just a figment of your own imagination, you won't believe me no matter what I say." He was pleading with me. Or was I pleading with myself? Was my dumb brain just trying to convince myself to hurt myself?

"You aren't real, or Ben isn't real, or this whole world isn't real. Or nothing is real. I'm being asked to decide which figment to believe."

"Does it really matter?" Hector shouted at me. "Look at you. You are a wreck. You aren't going to get better. There aren't any doctors here. There are no in-patient treatment programs you can try like last time. Who knows what pills Ben's been feeding you. You are just going to get worse and worse. You aren't happy. You don't have a life. You are ruining Ben's life. Wouldn't it be better to take that chance that I'm right? Your life here is painful and pointless. If I'm wrong, wouldn't it be better to just end it anyway?"

Was it worth it? Was it worth that chance? To get everything back I would have to give everything up. A leap of faith. That's what they call it, right? A leap of faith. A leap.

The chorus of voices returned. Louder now. Loud enough to hurt my ears. "Jump. Jump," they said.

"We'll catch you. You have to wake up. Elly, you have to wake up. There's only one way to wake up. It's all a dream. Jump." Strawberries. I couldn't even trust strawberries. I couldn't trust Ben. I couldn't trust Hector. I couldn't trust my own eyes and ears and dumb brain and the medicine that might not even be medicine and the books that might not even be books and the plants and the trees and the sky and the world that just might be pixels, but it also might be the only thing there is.

I got up out of my seat. Violently enough to actually turn over the table I was sitting at. A mug splashed and clattered to the floor. I stared at the shards. Do pixels break? The shapes of the pieces seemed so random. Computers can make random, right? Maybe. I don't know.

I started running. I just started running. Ben was walking down the driveway coming back from not being here with me. I flew right past him.

"Ell? Where are you going? Ell!?!"

I heard him continue to shout as I ran down the road. But I could also hear other voices, too. Some familiar to me, some not. Some loved. Some not.

Mom went first. "I know it's scary."

A woman's voice. "It seems scary."

A child's voice. "I don't even think I could do it."

My doctor. "But you have to be brave. You have to be strong."

I ran down the road with tears in my eyes. I couldn't see where I was going. I stumbled over a rock or something. I got to my knees and wiped my face with my sleeve. Hector was standing in front of me, appearing out of nowhere. "This is your last chance," he said. I swung my fists wildly at him as I ran past.

A child's voice. "Are you going to leave us forever?"

Mom? "Elly. I don't want to lose you forever."

The voices kept coming. "You don't want to lose us, do you? You have to remember us." Stop, stop. Leave me alone.

"You have to believe in us."

"We're not just ghosts."

"We're still alive."

"Don't let that monster lobotomize you. Please come home!"

"Come home!"

"You can do it, Aunt Elyse."

"Don't let that psycho win."

"Show him how strong you are."

"Jump."

"Jump."

"Jump!"

"Jump!"

Hector appeared right in front of me again. "Jump. We'll catch you."

The last thing I remember after that was everything fading out, and voices... millions of voices... all chanting, "Jump! Jump! Jump! Jump!..."

Still Day 214:

I was standing on a bridge. It was that same bridge where I'd been before, I think. I assume I ran there after seeing Hector. My memory isn't as good as it used to be. Sometimes things fade in and out. But I was definitely high up on a bridge. I know that much. The voices were still there, "Jump! Jump! Jump! Jump!"

I looked down at the water below. The river was moving faster than I remembered. You could see the white froth swirl about as the water churned violently. Everything blurred as my eyes filled with tears. I wiped my face with my sleeve and started to climb up over the railing. "Jump! Jump! Jump! Jump!"

Then a voice that was not the chorus appeared. Faintly, at first. It was hard to make out. But there, in the distance, was Ben, running down the road to the bridge. "Elyse! No, come back! I've got the strawberries! Don't do it, baby!" he said. Or at least he said something like that. I watched as he started to get closer. I put my leg over the railing. I looked down at the water below. The world, this world. What's in my head? What's real? What's unreal? What lies beyond? What came before? Time, space, everything. I couldn't tell what was real. I could never ever ever know what's real. Someone said your brain is forever trapped in the prison of your head. You'll only get a glimpse of what lies beyond by staring out the window of your eyes.

We live for meaning, for purpose, don't we? Isn't that the point of life? Find your purpose, find your calling, make the world a better place, live for your kids, lead a good life so you can get into heaven, lead a good life to reincarnate as royalty in the next cycle. If you don't have meaning, you don't have anything? You just have to figure out what's important to you, make something, anything, important to you. Focus on your career, your hobbies, your spouse, your god, *anything*; it doesn't matter what you focus on, but focus on something and live and die for it even if in the end it isn't true. Collect bottlecaps if you have to. The world is absurd, the world doesn't have inherent meaning, you have to make that meaning for yourself, right? You have to believe absolutely in something, right?

"No," I said.

Day 216:

I was ready by first light. The boat was small, but it was sturdy enough to survive the trip down river. There were some bags filled with food and stuff like that, but I figured I didn't need to bring that much. There'd be more stores filled with canned goods and what-not where I was going. I had a few things from my time here in the cabin; a couple of records I'd really liked, a favorite mug, some clothes I was comfortable in. My dog was already in the front, paws leaning over the railing, excited about seeing somewhere new.

Ben stood on the shore and watched me throw the last few bags into the boat. He had his hands in his pockets and his eyes didn't meet mine. "So. You are really going?" he said.

"I'm really going."

"You know I need you."

I wanted to reach out to him, but that would have only made it seem worse. "I know."

"What am I going to do without you?"

"Survive. Same as anyone else."

"Where are you going to go? There isn't anywhere to go."

"There's everywhere to go. That's the point."

"I'll never see you again?" his voice cracked a bit.

"No. You'll never see me again," I said, "I'm going to get in this boat and go down this river and end up somewhere in this very big world that isn't here. There's no way you could ever find me again... unless Hector was right. If this is a simulation, then you'll always know where I am, always be able to reach me.

But on the other hand, if this is the real world, you could search your entire life and never bump into me."

"Why are you doing this?" he knew why. He just didn't like it all that much.

"If I am not here to interact with you, and Hector was right, there's no reason for you to keep me here. Maybe you'll let me go, maybe you'll end the simulation, maybe I'll get back to the real world. The only way I can prove to myself that this isn't a simulation and you aren't a kidnapper is if you let me go forever."

"That's a sucky choice."

"I know. If Hector was wrong, I'm not being fair to you. And I will miss you, know that at least."

"Then why not just stay?" Why not stay? I could. Maybe.

"I've tried hard Ben. You know I've tried. But trying to impose a reason for living in this absurd corner of this dead, meaningless world is torturing me. Maybe it's because this world isn't real, maybe it's because my dumb brain is broken.

"But if nothing matters, then why not just stay? Even if I don't really matter to you," he said, obviously heartbroken.

"I've always looked to other people to protect me. Hector, you, random boyfriends, Mom. I've never been strong enough to stand on my own. Maybe that's what's been wrong all this time. Maybe if I'm strong enough to make it on my own, I'll prove something to myself."

I had been with Ben for what, like nine months by that point. I could read him. He was sad on the outside and sad on the inside, but also angry. "You're being selfish," he said. "By choosing to be alone, you're dooming me to the same fate." Was he angry because

I'd destroyed his carefully laid trap? Was he angry because I didn't need him, and in this crazy apocalypse he still, like all men, needed to be needed by someone? Was he only able to find meaning in life by mattering to someone else? He's right, without me to save, he wouldn't have a reason to live.

"I can't be your bottlecaps anymore, Ben. It's not enough for me to define my life in terms of being your reason to live. But you said yourself that even though we know we aren't going to be here forever, we have right now, and that's enough. Well, 'right now' is over. It had to happen someday, if not today, then someday. Shouldn't that be enough?"

He kicked at the sand. "Everything we built together is meaningless once you leave," he said, dejectedly.

"Look. You might not be alone. If we both survived then there must also be others out there who did." I said. "Maybe not in this city, but maybe in the next one, or the one after that. I'm going to go look for them. You should look for them too, baby. Get out of here, go somewhere else. Find those people, and you won't be alone. I have faith in you."

I got into the boat, and started to push at the sand with an oar. The bottom scraped against the shore for a few seconds, and then floated free. I stood, almost at attention, as I watched myself float further and further away from him. The last thing he said to me was, "At least you've got the dog. What am I left with?" Then he turned and walked silently back up to the cabin.

I watched him for as long as I could. The cabin got smaller and smaller as it slipped into the distance. A fog appeared and finally hid that little home from my view. I watched the trees slide by as the boat picked up some speed in the current. I sat down in the bow and started paddling.

I knew Hector was suddenly behind me, sitting in the stern. As I said before, I didn't have to look to know he was around, I could just sense him. I assumed he'd be back. The chorus of voices in my head had stopped once I'd made my decision up on that bridge. There was no point for them anymore. But I knew Hector wasn't gone for good.

Without turning around, I said to him, "I don't know if this is a simulation, or the real world. Maybe I'll never know."

Hector tried to respond. "Elyse, I...."

"...but simulation or not, this place *feels* real. This boat feels real. This paddle feels real. Even if it isn't reality, then it's good enough to live in. I wasn't doing that much with my old life anyway."

"So you are just going to stay here then?"

"Well, until Ben gets bored with me not talking to him and lets me go."

"What if he doesn't let you go?" Hector asked. "What if he just kills you?"

"Well, then at least I'll be out of my misery, won't I? But I know you, Hector. And if you are real, you'll never give up searching for me. I do hope you find me, I really do. And if you do, you can wake me up and I'll apologize for ever doubting."

Hector didn't respond right away. We paddled down the river in silence for a while. Eventually, I got tired of waiting for him. "But this world I'm in now is unforgiving," I said. "I can't live my life with doubt. I can't keep wondering if this is real. I can't keep waiting for someone to rescue me. I can't keep ignoring what's in front of my eyes in the hopes that I'll be transported to a better place someday. So, you have to go. You have to go and never come back. I know you are trying to comfort me and make sure I don't feel forgotten, but honestly I don't need to hope for a better world in order to live in this one. You have to go.

"If you come back, I'll know you are just a symptom of my madness. The real Hector will listen and understand, a hallucination won't. The only way you can really prove that you are real, that everything else I see and hear and feel isn't real, is to leave me alone forever.

"I'm strong enough to do this on my own Hector. I don't need you to rescue me. Be out there in your reality looking for me. But don't ever intrude into mine again. I've got my own private world to explore."

And like that, Hector was gone. I didn't need to look back at him. He didn't say anything more. He didn't need to save me. Maybe he finally understood that. Or maybe my dumb brain finally understood that I didn't need Hector to save me. That I didn't need Ben to save me. That, whether this world was real or unreal, whatever came before or existed beyond, I would be able to take what comes, minute by minute, day after day. And it didn't matter what happened. And I didn't need to find some hidden meaning to explain what I was doing here. This dead world was absurd, sure, but all I needed to do was sit back and enjoy the ride. Life doesn't need to have a meaning to be lived. It will be lived all the better if it has no meaning,

For a long time, I just sat in silence, listening to the currents lap up against the side of the boat, as I floated down the river into a thick fog.

About the Author

Dominic Peloso lives in Alaska, but in the rainy part, not the cold part.

Among the Ruins is his fourth prose novel. His first novel, City of Pillars, his second novel, Adopted Son, and his third novel, First World Problems in an Age of Terror and Ennui, are probably available in the same place you found this novel.

He is also the author of a depressing mixed-media comicstrip-esque photography project called Tiny Ghosts, which is found at: www.tinyghosts.com